Nightmares of an Appalachian Hillbilly

by

WD Phillips II

LAFAYETTE, TENNESSEE
deepreadpress@gmail.com

First Deep Read Press Edition.

Published in the United States of America

Edited by: Angie Novoa

Cover Design by: Kim Gammon

ISBN: 978-1-954989-60-3

Published by:
DEEP READ PRESS
Lafayette, Tennessee
www.deepreadpress.com
deepreadpress@gmail.com

This book is dedicated to Eva Phillips, Justin Hartsall, Jonathon Barett, Chris South, Bethe Webster, and Mike Russell. This book would not have been possible without your love and support.

Contents

Introduction

VERBAL histories and written words are like lighthouses of knowledge within a shadowed sea of ignorance. People throughout our known history have passed knowledge from generation to generation to eliminate ignorance. Some of those histories become muddled with superstition and things that could not be explained during earlier times, either through inexperience or scientific knowledge. However, the lesson within the story was the same: Avoid a potential danger. Other stories, even scientifically researched, are inexplicable and undefined by worldly knowledge that baffles those researchers. During those instances, the superstitions of spiritual nature or otherwise supernatural seem the most obvious choice in explaining those events.

I remember sitting with my father and grandfather on the porch of an old farmhouse in Cosby, Tennessee. We would whittle bits of wood while my dad, "Pop", and I would tell stories of the area and surrounding forests we were from. I remember some of them scaring the lights out of me but would still spark a bit of curiosity that would inspire the pursuit of seeking out the sites for myself. For better or worse, those experiences, either real or perceptually real, leave a mark on your mind that forces an individual to question the very definition of natural or supernatural.

Today was one of those rainy summer days. The wrap around porch with its tin roof allowed the drops of water to bang a rhythm on its surface that echoed around the occupants below. Three generations sat drinking sweet tea and enjoying one another's company, while the oldest began to tell stories from his childhood and more recent stories that were closer to his grandsons' day. Wind was gently blowing, providing a cooling breeze that misted and cooled the three with rainwater. Grandfather and father lit a cigarette, and Pop began to tell us the most fantastic string of stories that I remember to this day. Although some were nightmarish, they entertained my young mind and provided a strengthened bond between three generations. Pop's gravelly voice began to reverberate from the walls, creating another soothing and slightly mystical quality to the ambiance.

What's in There?

ALL manner of dreams begins the same way: Your body begins to relax, and your breathing patterns become slow and even. Your heart rate becomes measured, and after you have finally found that comfortable spot, you slowly drift to sleep. You become sandwiched between the softness of the pillow-topped mattress and warm soft sheets and blankets and nestle further into its comforting bliss. It begins with a brief blackness, then what seems like a fantastical movie starts to stream through your mind's eye. However, as we age and the gravity of people and their opinions weigh us down, our dreams become less fantastical in nature and the belief in its magic slowly begins to fade.

It was a hot summer afternoon, in June, at the base of the Smokey Mountains on my inherited property in Tennessee. Nestled between mountains within a valley and surrounded by a creek that is fed by an underground and mountain spring, it runs all year with clear water, full of aquatic plant and animal life. The peaceful landscape of gently rolling hills with groves of dogwoods, black walnut, poplar, white oak, maple, and birch provided such a veil of shade as to reflect the hot sun's heat away from the ground beneath them. A slight breeze blew as J, a longtime friend, and I were sitting beneath two large cedars beside the creek and enjoying the wind as we puffed on our herbal cigarette. We were discussing life in general. Nothing out of the ordinary until he stopped mid puff and leaned forward, squinting his eyes as if to strain to peer through the tree line on the opposite side of the creek. He tapped my arm and pointed in the direction of eleven o' clock from where we were seated.

"It's a portal to the faerie world," said J with a smile, jokingly still pointing in the direction he wanted me to look. After some searching, I saw it. Flanked by two large boulders, and grown into a large hill, is a huge white oak. Within its center is an ovular hole that is approximately four feet in length and one foot in width. It is deep and dark, from our vantage point, so that its contents could not be seen. We spoke for several more hours, joked, and conversed for a while longer, enjoying the Appalachian landscape and the perfect day. As J began to leave and I was walking down my quarter mile driveway, I spied again the tree J had referred earlier and wondered, "What's in there?"

I remember, when my cousin and I were younger, we played all over the surrounding mountains and forests as if they were our playgrounds. We saw things with our imaginations and lost ourselves within that magical world. With sword and spear we killed dragons and marauding orcs and goblins. We chased hordes of enemies far from our families' lands with vigorous youth. One day we chased a particularly quick-running ogre across the swollen creek, after a spring storm, and into the field on the other side of the creek. Suddenly the ogre took an unexpected turn and ran into the large portal within the oak tree and vanished. Try as I might, I could not convince my cousin to venture into the portal and scout the faerie land first. No amount of convincing would do it, so I resigned to go with him. We got a few feet from the darkened entrance when another thunder crack scared our imaginative young minds, and we bolted back toward the trailer in which his family lived. We never saw what was in the tree. As youth, we peered into an abyss that was full of true and real dangers, and we dared not go back. The magic and our dreams survived the day, however, and we considered that a win.

Our adventures after the portal incident became legendary, but slowly the landscape began to change as the sculptor labored and cleaned until the forest became a yard. During this period, the magical creatures we used to hunt, and battle became less and less observed. We noticed that they came to the entire area no longer and the ogre that we had chased only a few years ago had never come out again. As the rivers of time continued to slowly flow, as it tends to do in your youth, our adventures had changed to walnut wars, grape vine swings, and bicycle rides. We observed wild and untamed flora and fauna and weird and unexplained structures in the deep woods. I heard later about the ritualistic gatherings that were sometimes held in those places and was told to avoid them. During this time, my father had fought the enchanted forest back and made a large yard and moved a double wide trailer under the remaining trees' green canopies.

The sun's rays crested the Appalachian Mountain range again and again. Summers were becoming noticeably shorter, and time seemed to accelerate. Magic within dreams, during these times, had matured into a more primal nature. It was one where the female body had replaced dreams of magical powers and the ability to fly. Powers of persuasion and physical prowess replaced dragon's breath and ogre axes as weapons to, metaphorically, combat this foe. Chasing girls became the primary pursuit, instead of defending our homes from the bloodthirsty ogres of yesteryear. Another form of magic showed itself in a spectacular manner as well during this time. A savior. A communicator. A way to express myself that sent those around into a world of peace with a musical story. During summer nights, as the magic of playing music with friends and family receded, my father and I passed a joint while watching the lightning bugs and wondered again at the Oak tree, "What's in there?"

It came to me as it comes to us all eventually, the graduation of high school and entering adulthood. I joined the military and did not see the Portal in the Large Oak for some time after leaving. The magic that I once had was now all but forgotten, and was replaced by the worries of adulthood, being in battle, and the responsibility to my brothers and sister in arms. Magic no longer visited my dreams if dreams ever came. Dreams that I had, even in my early adolescence, seemed to fade in a lackluster mire of self-disapproval and the discouraging words of my mother. Yet, during the short times I visited my home and father and son, would again watch the lightning bugs and my eyes would find that oak and wonder, "What's in there?"

After the military and a divorce, I moved back home to this little spot in Tennessee. I missed the mountains I called home with their misty blankets and serene views. After some time, I chased a dream and found small success. I found, during this achievement, I should have followed my dream and held some of the magic I lost in my youth instead of listening to words of discouragement. During this time, the magic took another form by way of the emotional energy that is given and received while being on stage and observed by quite a few people. The best way it could be described is like an extended orgasm that lasts hours after the last note is played. Dreams returned after this discovery, and they were lined with part of the youthful magic that I experienced when I was younger. During these days, the oaken portal morphed from a portal to the faerie into something a bit more sinister. Something that screamed defiance and fearful promises that made one consider double locking their door and taking every precaution necessary. The nature of the past "faerie portal" darkened and changed into the form of a rumored murder hole.

Many people, like myself, joined the military fresh out of high school and eventually had to go to combat in one theatre or another. There were many thieves that were roaming around these hills during those times. It was rumored that one such thief had broken into one of the other veterans' homes. This person tracked the thief to his home and threatened him harm if he ever returned. It was rumored that the portal in the large oak was used to hide bodies or mutilated human parts, bringing the darker magic of fear into the heart of the listener of the stories of a serial killer that was never caught. Oddly, or imaginatively, on warmer days and seasons while my father and I watched the cows and horses that populated the field beyond, I noticed the animals avoided the opening in the large oak. I wondered then as in my youth, "What's in there?"

Several years passed by and the magic that I once experienced was passed to my daughter. All the hope and joy that I once knew, I saw reflected in her eyes and personality. She is a blonde-haired angel that brought a peace to my soul even during the darkened wonderings and dreams that had tortured me for years. As she danced in the middle of the moss floored dogwood grove, I noticed again the hole in the large oak and after so many years I still wondered, "What's in there?"

Still more time passed, and my father died in the fall of the year. Dreams come even less frequently now. Worry and doubt have beaten and torn away any shred of the existence of the magic that once may have been. The magic was gone as my father had left this world behind. I recalled the conversation, on that June day, about the faerie portal. Or was it a murder hole? During that conversation he described what sounded like a large black squirrel running across the field and into the oaken hole.

As I stand on my inherited back porch and gaze across the yard I have begun to further sculpt for my daughter, as my father left me, I see that old oaken portal. The warm summer morning dew sends sparkles of crystalline reflections across the emerald lawn and leaves of the trees. I drank my coffee and put out my cigarette and turned to open the sliding door and put on my shoes. I left the house and traversed the quarter mile driveway to cross the creek and into the field on the other side. Following the very same trail my cousin and I had chased the evil ogre back to the realm of the faerie, I slowly crossed the field and saw the oak loom on the horizon. Trepidation crept into my mind. An anxiousness began to come over me as I slowly closed the distance toward the oak, and I asked myself, "Is this a magical portal, a murder hole, or something's nest?" With fear came that youthful magic of an overactive imagination. My senses heightened. I strained to hear each sound and notice everything within sight. My eyes darted from shadow to shadow, remembering how coyotes had traversed the area the night before, and although nocturnal, could hide within the large opening. I slowed my pace and tried to spy anything within its darkened depts. I came closer, now only twenty feet from the left most boulder and the wind began to blow. It was a nice summer breeze that carried the sweet smell of honeysuckle in an aromatic relaxing manner. I inched closer, beginning to experience an unexplained fear and spied a large stick at my feet that I picked up to use as a potential club. I stared into the blackness. Nothing within moved and all was seemingly still inside, judging by the levels of blackness and shadows cast by the shining sun. I came within five feet and was finally able to peer inside and there it was. The hollowed out, and partially rotted, interior of a large white oak. No portal to another world of fantastical and wonderful beings. No murder hole used to dump bodies. No rare squirrel nest that was evident within either. It was just a large, cavernous opening in a huge oak tree.

After turning and walking back across the field and toward my house, I came to the stark realization that it finally happened. All the magic that was in the world was now gone to me and was replaced by the stark and depressing reality of adulthood. Dreams no longer come and large aspirations are tempered and replaced by the responsibilities that come with age and having children. I am not sad at this discovery, but I mourn its loss and have found a light that maintained the warmth of hope. Maybe with that light of hope, we, as adults, can find the magic we once had as children to dream again, and follow their coordinates back to the road of their destiny and ask, "What's in there?"

Devil in the Mists

GROWING up in the Appalachian Mountain range in east Tennessee, you hear a lot of superstition and folklore about a variety of things: Devils, witches, demons, and other savage and brutal monsters that roam about in the deep woods. Such is the story of the "Bogard Booger." There are several different versions of the story. One being a large, mutated cat that screams like a woman when hunting you. Another version includes the horrible death of a native American that belonged to a long dead nomadic tribe. No matter the version you choose to listen to, or believe, both have familiarizing attributes that spur the imagination into wild and wondrous fantasies. Unfortunately, those fantasies quickly shade the sun with their dark presence and instill a modicum of fear within the listener. Yet, fear is a funny thing. It can make adrenaline pump through the body and allow for increased abilities that one would not normally have. Fear can be a debilitating thing that causes loss of bowel and urinary control, forcing individuals into a fetal position of quivering anxiety. This unique effect from that emotion is what disturbed three young boy cousins of age ten one summer night.

It was a warm summer's day in July at his grandmother's house. It was a small three-bedroom home that was within a community of middle-class people. The small home's exterior was made from red brick and had a dark colored shingle roof with a car port to the right of the front door. His grandmother had hired a neighbor to aid in her lawn care to his fathers' new shift at work. He had begun working evenings and attending school during the night to pay off his newly acquired property.

The boy waited patiently in the living room, watching cartoons and eating cereal with his grandmother. After about two hours, or three Saturday morning cartoons worth, the boy heard his father rouse and begin to stumble toward the bathroom. The boy knew better than to approach his father before coffee. Not that the man was mean to him or anything. It was just that he was not as fun to annoy before that first nip of caffeine. This day, he chose to sit with him and watch cartoons quietly. Back in those days, cartoons would play on every basic network channel for hours, and father and son watched them through.

It was just about one in the afternoon when father and son loaded in the truck and headed east toward the mountains. The old nineteen seventy-six model Ford pickup absolutely loved gas, the father would always complain, but he only looked over and smiled at his son as hard rock music blared from the truck's stereo system. They listened to the "Hells Bells" album, by AC/DC until arriving at a small gas station that also had a restaurant in the building. They went in and got their cheeseburger specials and resumed their trip toward their property in the mountains.

They enjoyed the scenery and overall pleasantness of the day. The way the wind felt warm and comforting flowing through the driver and passenger windows forming a wind tunnel that effectively cooled off the truck's passengers as they traveled. The two-lane road wound on with the mountains in front of you, blocking all view of anything else. Although not the tallest mountain range, there are parts that climbed high. Slowly the father applied pressure to the brake and began to slow to make a right-hand turn onto another paved road.

They turned right and drove past a trailer park and over a bridge that rose above a creek that often swelled over it in a mighty current and was regularly stocked with trout upstream. They continued the windy road until they made a sharp right-hand turn and finally came to an old gravel road that was flanked by an apple orchard. The boy loved coming here. He could explore the whole wild countryside and never have to come inside the house. Especially on days like today. His childlike eyes stared around in wonderment at the possibilities of today's events when his eyes caught sight of the tent in the covered bed of the pickup.

"Are we going camping today, Dad?" the boy asked in wonderment and surprise. His father did not make the amount of money his mother did, but he allowed his son to be himself and guided him instead of lecturing.

14

"Well, your cousins, Scott and Ed, are coming and I figured I'd take y'all swimmin' atter awhile," the boy's father said in that particular Tennessee drawl that the boy had inherited, and parked the truck onto his newly acquired land.

The man had a vast majority of the property cleaned off and most of all the trees he wanted gone were cut and logged. However, there were still two thirds of the property that remained untouched. At the foot of the Smokey Mountains, there was wildlife that was known to migrate through the area and use it as a hunting ground. The man's son used to wonder why his father would carry his shotgun with him, but he soon let those questions rest as others took their place. They enjoyed the cheeseburger meal under a grove of black walnut trees that encircled a moss-covered clearing. Around one side of the glen runs a clear and wide creek that provides a relaxing sort of rhythm to add to the scenery's ambiance.

After a few moments passed by and the birds and other wildlife were in their song and dance routines, two youthful voices crashed through the tranquility of the forest. A tall lanky youth beside his shorter and stumpy cousin walked toward the father and son as they sat watching their arrival. Salutations and greetings were exchanged, and the trio ran off into the woods while the father rose to begin his work. "Make sure you come when I call, son," the man called after his retreating boy.

"I will, Dad," replied the youth, his voice trailing off into the hills. The trio played in the hills for what seemed like only moments. The largest of the three displayed his father's old army knife. The father had allowed his son to use the blade, knowing his boy enjoyed building forts and things of that nature. He was also aware that his son knew the proper use of a knife of which he had instructed him in handling it safely. At that moment, a scream sounded deep in the eastern woods which froze the boys in place for a few moments. After minutes of silence the boys shrugged off that jolt of fear and resumed their play.

After, what seemed like, a few moments longer the boys heard the father/uncle call for them. They raced down the mountainside and came to the property of which they were called. The man loaded up the boys in the back of the pickup and removed the cover over the trucks bed to allow the boys to ride in the open air. He then got into the truck and opened the rear sliding window to allow the children to hear the music, checked to make sure the boys were okay, and then started the truck to traverse the dirt road back to the main road. He drove the children to a national park that is located just past a paper mill and off the I-40. The water there is crisp with mountain run-off water giving it a cold temperature that is both refreshing and forces the breath from your body. The boys did not care. They traversed the rocky banks toward the large and clear creek with youthful exuberance and plunged into its cold depths. The trio played and splashed and rode the smaller rapids until the father called them to leave. They left the water smiling and laughing with blue lips, chattering teeth, and chill bumps on their arms and legs. The father/uncle smiled at the boys' youthfulness and took them to the rest area on the other side of the bridge to dry off and change clothes. After the boys completed this task, the father drove to the supermarket to purchase the normal camping cuisine of hotdogs and smores with sodas thrown in for good measure. They left the market and traveled the winding country roads back to the property they had earlier left.

The sun was shining brightly but had begun its descent toward the western mountain line. The father started a small cooking fire in a tiny Webster grill and began unloading the camping gear from the truck. The three children played in the woods until the man called them once again. The trio came through the woods on the western side and grabbed hotdogs to quickly scarf down, but as they turned to leave, Buck heard a snap from a twig on his left, in the direction of the wilder area of the forest. A slight chill ran through his spine, but he shrugged it off with a laugh and ran back toward the western side of the woods with the other two. He failed to notice the flock of birds that scattered in the direction of the noise moments after he turned and joined his cousins.

An hour later, the lightning bugs began their dance among the trees' canopies and the creek banks. They sparkled around the freshly mowed grass and within the denser woods beyond. Buck's father started a campfire, and his brother began making smores for the boys. The younger trio gathered around the two older men and took their share of the sweet treat with a smile and sat around the fire in a circular fashion. The moss-covered ground provided a cushy seat, and they sat cross legged on its comfortable green surface. The two older men smiled at one another, and Buck's father asked," Do you want to hear some stories?" The trio nodded eagerly, and the two older men sat down and peered worriedly behind them in the eastern section of the woods briefly before turning back toward the children.

"Now, I don't know of any ghost stories off tha top o' muh head, but I do remember a rumor Granny told us when we were kids," Buck's father looked at his brother and he solemnly nodded his head. "I think she said that it was back in the seventeen hundreds?" He turned and looked at his brother in askance, of whom grunted his agreement. He had already drunk three too many and had that telltale trail of drool forming a stream of saliva down the curve of his chin. Buck's father rolled his eyes and turned back to the children to resume his tale. As he opened his bearded mouth to speak, his gaze wandered toward the fire that was beginning to burn low. He looked around and found a log that was a size that suited him and threw it into the fire. His tall form took quick and long strides back toward the log pile to prepare for the eventuality of the fire burning low, and he returned quickly to tell his young audience about the old story.

The man bent down with creaking knees to sit on a fallen poplar tree and began his tale. "In the seventeen hundreds, when the settlers were passing through this area and headed west, there was this Native woman in the forest, picking berries and herbs to aid her nomadic tribe in their trip north. It was during the end of the summer when it happened. Three settlers came upon this lady in this area of the woods. When they saw her, it was the first time they had ever seen anything like her. So unlike the women from home. So exotic and wild. So different from the tame ladies across the ocean. A terrible light entered the eyes of the three men as they gazed longingly at the wild and savage woman. She froze like a deer when she saw them approach her. She had never seen men such as these, with their shiny shirts and pale skin, but she knew the look that burned in their eyes. It was the same look she observed in invading warriors' eyes. The eyes that burned with lust and the desire for rape.

"To her credit, she fought the best she could, against three men, but ultimately after they finished whatever carnal pleasures, they wanted they beat her. They thought her dead when they left her. She was still. She did not breathe. They killed several other braves and people on their way west, I heard, but they did not kill her.

"She awoke, a few days later facing extreme starvation and loss of blood. When she came to this realization, she began crawling back toward the area she remembered her tribe to be. She only made it about twenty yards, when she spied through hazed eyes, smoke in the distance and the smell of fresh blood. She had to get to food, so she crawled on, but her body had begun to give itself out. When she came to this understanding, she began looking for anything to eat and her eyes fell on a newly dead Native warrior. She crawled slowly toward the body, regretting and loathing the thing she was about to do. She found the warrior's blade and began to carve the flesh from his leg. I have heard that some believe you become cursed if you devour human flesh, but anyway, she eventually died from the wounds caused by her attackers. However, her ancestors saw her crime of eating the flesh of man and cursed her. Granny said that sometimes, you can hear her scream throughout the hills at night. She said if you hear her, to cover your eyes and ears or she'll come and eat you." Buck's father finished his story and smiled at the trio of boys, "Y'all ain't skeered, are ye?" he asked as mockingly country as possible. He put one more log onto the fire and turned and motioned to his brother, indicating his turn.

"Yea. I heard her tell that one, but that ain't the one I believe," he said, looking at Buck's dad with a sneer and crooked look. "I heard it was a huge mountain lion, or a panther, that had decided to use this area and all the way Sevierville to hunt." That last bit was more effective than the detailed story of Buck's father. They had been roaming the woods for hours today and heard the scream that Buck's father referred to. Could they be the same? The trio began to get a bit scared. Their imaginations began to work in overdrive as things began to take on attributes of fantastical and amazing things, driven with fear, making the forest a playground for all sorts of monsters and demons.

The two adults had had enough and told the three youngsters' good night and walked westward toward Buck's uncle's house. The three kids stayed awake a bit longer, regaling one another with more stories. Scott left the tent shortly after Eddie had finished his story of a serial killer that was loose in the area, killing with a knife. So, when Scott left, Eddie and Buck hatched a plan. Buck would leave the tent and wait a few moments after Scott came back in. After the wait, he would kick at the fire and act like a killer was walking around the tent.

The time had come, and the plan was executed as planned, which effectively scared Scott and the other two, as well, due to the story telling. As the fire began to burn lower and the boys began to settle down and snicker in their sleeping bags, a mist began to slither into the wooded valley. Eventually, due to the song of crickets and other wildlife coupled with the rhythm of the creek, the boys fell asleep within the tent. After a few moments Buck was startled awake by that same chilling feeling he had felt earlier, and then he heard a twig snap in the eastern and more wild side of the forest behind the tent.

As quickly as his ears registered the snap of the twig, he recalled his drunken uncle's tale of the panther that was using this area as its hunting ground. The campfire outside had burned low and was primarily embers, and his cousins had cocooned themselves around the flashlights, so Buck gripped his knife tightly and unzipped the tent. He did this as lightly and discreetly as possible while holding the blade at the ready. His heart pounded in his ears as the zipper slowly reached the desired position and he peered through the opening. Upon seeing nothing, he poked his head out and gazed around the dimly lit area but saw nothing. Again, there came a snap and a slight rustle behind the tent and Buck jumped backward into the tent and waited a few moments. Upon hearing nothing he tightened his grip on the blade, and it gave him confidence. He cautiously poked his head out to inspect the area again and noticed that the fire had gotten a bit lower, but the full moon brightened the area well. Buck exited the tent slowly, the hair on his neck and arms standing on end. A wind blew at that moment and the remaining fire died in a tired puff of exhaustion from this evening's work, diminishing the remainder of Bucks firelight.

Buck was already checking the perimeter of the surrounding forest before the remaining flame puffed out, however. As he looked northeasterly toward the hills beyond, he saw a flash of large green luminous eyes staring at him from the woods. Just as the fire flared before dying with the blowing wind, the eyes flashed red. That is all it took for Buck. He launched the blade in the direction of the eyes, and dove into the tent and zipping it before crawling into his sleeping bag and covering his head. The next morning, Buck's father came to wake the boys for breakfast and Buck relayed what happened the night before to his father and uncle.

"You threw away the only weapon you had," joked Buck's uncle, causing everyone to laugh.

Buck laughed nervously and quickly finished his breakfast to leave with his father. However, it would be a day or two later that Buck's father found the thrown combat knife in that wild edge of the eastern woods. The thing that astounded, and worried, Buck's father is that he found his knife laying only inches from a large paw print.

Thing in the River

ALL throughout the world there are many stories about the Earth's watery depths and the things that dwell in them. Some are based on rumors or sightings of beasts that live in that watery world and prey upon unwary visitors to its domain. Other stories take on more a supernatural nature. Where superstition of burning or burying remains of loved ones could result in their untimely return and could cause their spirit to become vengeful in a manner that will cause harm to those they view as a threat. Of course, there are scientific explanations as well that cease all manner of speculation and questioning. What information does the search for truth hold? Will finding the answer increase your knowledge, or will the search itself provide the information you truly seek? These questions are what led an amateur investigator to more questions as she searched out the rumors of the thing that lived in the Pigeon River.

Erin was visiting her grandparents in East Tennessee for the summer. She was just entering high school and still trying to find herself within the whirlwind of emotions that occur with adolescence. She is a tall girl that appeared a little too thin. Her metabolism made it near impossible for her to gain weight and she was consistently berated and called anorexic or some other terrible name that children call other children. Visiting this area was a refreshing change from the frozen personalities of the people she lived around in Wisconsin. People in this area were generally nice to everyone but did not fully accept outsiders until they got to know you. Erin's parents were from this area, born and raised and everyone in the small town knew them. Every summer she would visit her grandparents' neighbors and listen to their stories. She was beginning to find that she liked to find the truth from stories that were told, giving her the idea to try for a reporting position with her school paper when school recommenced.

One story caught her interest. She sat with Deborah and listened to the tale of an Olympic swimmer that had drowned in the river that ran not but two blocks and across the road from where Erin sat. The story was that the woman was swimming with several other teenage kids in the river one summer day. It was, apparently, around one o'clock in the afternoon when the girl stopped swimming laps mid stroke and began to tread water with a surprised look on her face. Deborah stated that the look of confusion quickly turned to shock then fright. Then, in the blink of an eye, the girls' hands flew up and her blonde ponytail trailed behind her rapidly plunging body below the river's surface. The older woman's eyes went vague as she sipped her tea on the tin covered porch, as if what she remembered disturbed her, and shook her head to clear away the vile memory. Her poof of bluish-gray hair flew about in a barely visible jiggle that reminded Erin of a humorous looking jelly mold, and she snickered slightly at her own humor.

Deborah went on for a while longer. She told Erin several other stories of people going missing in the river on the other side of the road. This last bit intrigued Erin, and she began to wonder if anyone else in the neighborhood knew anything of it. She resigned herself to inquire more on this issue from her grandparents and others tomorrow, for the sun's rays had dimmed and the lightning bugs had started their dance. As she rose from her seat on Deborah's porch, Erin heard the boyish laughter from the kids across the street. She smiled and waved at the three who ran under a large pine tree catching the phosphorescent bugs.

Her grandparents' house was down the street and six houses on the right side of the road. It, like many in the community, was a dark red brick house with a dark shingled roof. She enjoyed the cookie-cutter community, not because of anything other than the people that inhabited it. Everyone that lived here was kind and respectful. They threw up a hand in response to salutation or to give one. This knowledge warmed her soul as the soft summer breeze cooled her skin and comforted her mind and forced a smile to cross her face. Still, she pondered on Ms. Deborah's stories of all those that had died mysteriously on that stretch of the Pigeon River.

She finally arrived at her grandparents' house and turned the knob to open the door. She walked in and removed her shoes due to the light off-white carpet. Various figurines made of porcelain adorned multiple shelves, and cabinets were scattered throughout the living room. A large entertainment center sat against the eastern most wall that almost totally blocked any sight of the wall behind it due to the aid of the television that sat atop it. A recliner sat next to a large window that presented a view of the front yard and the road that bisected the community. A coffee table sat toward the center of the living room and a couch that was tan in color sat against that northern wall with a tapestry of Jesus feeding the masses behind it.

Erin's grandparents were in the kitchen beyond, sitting down to dinner when she rounded the corner and entered to join them. She sat in the chair opposite her grandmother and to the right of her grandfather, facing the window and the fading sun's rays. As they ate, Erin inquired her grandmother of Ms. Deborah's creditability, and her answer was not one that Erin hoped for. Apparently, the woman had the reputation of being a habitual liar and nothing she said could be trusted. Erin's grandfather asked why the line of questioning, and Erin revealed the stories that she had shared with Ms. Deborah earlier. Grandfather nodded his head and confirmed the tales. He even made Erin aware of the public records that would confirm the story. They made small talk for the remainder of the meal and Erin excused herself from the table to get ready for bed and resume her investigation of the mysterious disappearances of all those people. Her sleep was troubled that evening as she lay in bed, wondering how these disappearances happened and where the lost were now. She resigned to first question some more of the folks she knew had lived in this community for some time. Then, she would go to the small-town courthouse and refer the information to public records and compare. Smiling at the possibility of solving a mystery, she fell fast asleep anxious to begin the next day.

The next morning, she rose before her grandparents, eager to begin her quest to uncover the unknown. She ate some cereal and watched the morning cartoon show on channel thirty-nine. Cartoons did not last as long on weekdays, so she used this knowledge to schedule the best time for her to properly visit people. She completed some small chores around the house and looked at the clock, noting the time of ten-fifteen. She said goodbye to her grandparents and made them aware of whom she was visiting before departing. There were kidnappers running rampant during these days in the late eighties. Kids were being taught how to recognize dangerous people and how to avoid them.

Erin spent the next few hours visiting the neighborhood and making mental notes of the four people that had gone missing, and of the double suicide that had occurred several years before Erin was even born. She left the Maxwells' house last and began walking to her grandparents. It was almost dinner time again and the three cousins were being their rambunctious selves, making the best of their summer. She arrived and went in to join her grandparents for dinner and explained all that she had inquired of that day. Both grandparents nodded their ascent to the gathered information and agreed to drive the fourteen-year-old to the courthouse to continue her investigation. The excitement in their granddaughter's eyes and voice spurred their approval, and they were proud of her ambition and interest in discovering the truth. In addition, they had often had the same questions but never had the time to pursue them.

The next morning, Grandfather woke Erin, and they got ready to go to the courthouse and resume her investigation. On their way, they stopped at Hardee's for biscuits and gravy and continued their way when finished. They drove on the main highway until the road came to a four-way red light. The light turned green after a moment, and the pair continued to drive down to the next red light in their nineteen eighty-one Monte Carlo.

The car was light blue and without a muffler, which made it rumble like a train down the road. They had their windows rolled down and enjoyed the wind that blew and circulated as they approached the red light at the end of a T-intersection that faced a railroad track. Just beyond the railroad tracks wound the same

Pigeon River that was discussed with her grandparents' neighbors. This was the area where they said the double suicide happened. The story went the pair were of different races. The woman was white, and the man was black. During those days, in this small town, and even some now, interracial relationships were frowned upon, and they were bullied and accosted until they both leapt into the river hand in hand. Their bodies were found some miles down the river and a monument was rumored to be erected to honor their memory in the form of a white cross on a mound of stacked rocks. The light turned to green, and the pair made a right-hand turn and head toward the courthouse. They passed multiple small shops, bars, and a movie rental place before coming to a stop at another red light at a four-way stop. Just ahead and to the right sat their destination, but to the left of the railroad tracks and far ahead of her position, Erin spied the white cross monument. Her excitement mounted as the light turned green and they continued to their destination and parked their car.

Erin went into the courthouse unaccompanied and made her way to the county clerk. She received the files she sought from the dark-haired older lady from behind the desk and turned to sit at a desk to peruse them. She found several missing persons cases that involved a swimming disappearance and noted that they numbered at five. Five unexplained disappearances in the last twenty years, and a double suicide that happened first. She remembered the old superstition of spirits and what happened when ashes were spread in water or bodies were buried around water. It was the superstition that the spirit of the recently deceased would return to the land of the living as a restless spirit. She discounted that thought with a laugh and, gaining the knowledge she sought, she returned the files to the clerk and left to join her grandfather that was patiently waiting by his car. They left the courthouse and began their way back toward Grandfather's house. They passed several red lights that adorned this area of town before finally making a right-hand turn by an old Victorian house that is huge and run-down. That house was beautiful when it was first built, I bet, thought Erin, enjoying the warm breeze on her youthful face. As they drove on, her eyes began to linger on the river that ran perpendicular to the road of which they traveled. It was the same river that had claimed the lives of seven victims. It was beautiful to look at. Its white rapids that splashed over large rocks and its clear surface enticed any to jump into its cooling waters, but those sinister questions still lingered on Erin's mind as they made the left-hand turn into Grandfather's neighborhood. The pair arrived at their home and went inside and grabbed a quick lunch. Erin went over her findings with Grandmother and came to the decision to go and observe the river for the next few days during differing hours to hopefully glimpse something that was potentially fantastical, or horrible.

Erin sat at the riverside for many hours over the next few days and witnessed nothing substantial. During the morning hours, she viewed wild ducks and fish at play and disturbing the river's surface. In the afternoons, she resolved to float on the river itself in a yellow raft she had purchased from Wal-Mart and paddled the length of the river that ran adjacent to the road to town, but saw nothing fantastical in nature.

She had given up hope on the last night of her summer stay with her grandparents, when she finally thought she saw something. It was dusk and the sun was rapidly beginning to set. The mosquitoes had taken to using Erin as the gourmet meal they had awaited since hatching, which led her to begin gathering her things. As she reached for her lantern to begin her walk, she noticed a ripple that danced across the river's surface, and she looked out over the water to locate its source. A few moments passed by, and she noticed what appeared to be a large log half-floating down the river. Erin shrugged her shoulders and began to turn and walk toward Grandpa's house when she saw the 'log' quickly plunge beneath the water's surface and disappear. She stood and watched in amazement, wondering if the log would resurface. When it did not, she began to get closer to the river and follow its current to find the log. When she came within four feet of the river's edge, she saw a ripple disturb the waters again and turned her light to face the water and saw nothing but the accumulation of bugs gathering about her lantern. She took another step toward the river's edge and heard a splash ten feet to her left and behind her and she bolted across the road, past the church, and to her grandpa's front door before she registered how fast her legs had brought her.

Just like every evening this summer, Erin told her grandparents of her findings and, most especially, the frightful event that had just occurred. Still a little shaken, she went and bathed and went to bed. Grandfather took her to the airport to catch her flight back to Wisconsin the next day. She hugged and kissed her grandparents goodbye and cried tears of happiness and loss because she knew she would miss them. She would see them next summer, but she hated this part. Her grandfather gave her this morning's newspaper and they parted ways.

On her flight Erin opened her paper and stared wide eyed at its top story. The headline read, "A body was found just two miles downriver from Grace Baptist church...." It went on with all sorts of details, but what caught her attention was they found the body at the bottom of the white cross burial mound. It had large puncture wounds on both sides of her leg that indicated and resembled a large reptilian bite.

The Barn

WHEN we are children and our imaginations run wild, it is difficult to discern between reality and dream. I remember growing up in a trailer park in East Tennessee that spurred the most fantastical and terrifying imaginings that I experienced in my youth. I often wonder if that had to do with being brought up in an abusive household, and my mind using these fantasies and imagined horrors to aid in coping with those tumultuous times. As it was, I made good friends within that little low-income community. We shared each other's lower-class standards with a joyful ignorance that maintained a shared happiness within the group. During the summer one evening, one of our little groups would stumble upon something that caused us to remain indoors and move to another home.

It was the summer of nineteen ninety-two when my friend Josh and I were riding through the neighborhood on our bikes and preparing for a ramp jump that would shred our innocence. School had just ended, and the students began their summer break. Rick had an amazing year and was just about to start seventh grade the following year, but at the end of May he had three or four months to enjoy before worrying about anything of an academic nature. His stepsister had begun driving that year, and her boyfriend would come and play pick pickup games with Rick and his other friends in the trailer park. Most of Rick's friends were older than he by three years, making it difficult for him to relate to those of his same age. Josh was about the closest to his age within the group of children that played together. They would have basketball games at Rick's; softball games in the field at Chris'; play hide and seek, explore the surrounding area, or ride their bikes.

Today, as Rick left the confines of the bus and began to walk the remaining way home, he pondered where his stepsister was. Rick had elected to ride the bus to make out with his girlfriend. It was a puppy love that would not last, but neither child really thought of that. The two loved each other's company and usually got lost in youthful passions and dreams that never gained any substance. His stepsister was spending some unsupervised time with her current boyfriend. She had begun to get a bit miffed at Rick due to the fact her boyfriend and his friends seemed to enjoy hanging out with Rick more than she. They would join Rick and his friends' pickup games and would usually ignore the female they came to visit. This thought made Rick laugh out loud as he ran down the hill to the little racetrack that encircled a swimming pool in the front portion of the trailer park of which Rick lived.

They lived in the middle trailer on the first row that faced the highway and the swimming pool. Rick's grandparents had lived in a house that overlooked the trailer park, but new road construction tore down their house and forced them to move. Rick missed seeing his grandfather every day, but all the neighborhood friends he had accumulated filled the loneliness caused by his grandparents' move. Rick had lived with them during the formative years of his life. His mother had dropped him off at their home on a mountaintop on the families' property known as "Green Corner" until his father returned from the military at age five. She would leave him for months on end with his grandparents. During those days, cell phones were not yet invented, and the Internet was in its earliest stages of conception, which left either letters or a landline as methods of correspondence. Rick would not hear from his mother. He remembered asking his grandfather when Mommy was coming back, but he would only reply, "I don't know son." This began a chasm in Rick and his mother's relationship. Rick respected and loved his mother, but his stepfather was beating those respectful and loving feelings from him. Rick's mother would do nothing as the stepfather would pick him up by the throat to choke him, punch him around a bit, or hit him with some other blunt object. Most of the time the stepfather would do this while Rick's mother was working. In the earlier days of that relationship, Rick would tell his mother of her then boyfriend's actions. She would call Rick a liar and say, "We don't tell lies," or just sweep the information under the rug and be forgotten, which would almost always result in another beating. As a result, Rick would perform poorly in school and would stay in his room or outside with his friends until dark. He would do anything to avoid the two people who often mistreated him or ignored him completely.

Through his musings, Rick finally reached the door to the tan trailer that was his home. The old man that lived to the left of Rick's home waved and smiled at the boy and Rick walked over and sat with the ninety-year-old man and talked. He enjoyed his talks with the elderly man. His name was Haskell. He was like an old library that was full of fantastic stories from the past that taught Rick a lot about how to be a moral person. Rick stayed with Hack until his sister finally pulled into her parking spot and began getting out of her car. Rick said goodbye to Hack and walked over to meet with his stepsister and enter their home. The pair joked amicably while Rick put away his school items and prepared a snack for the day's coming adventures when there came a knock at the door.

He peered through the door window and saw his friend Josh that lived up the road about a mile in a single-wide trailer with his father. He was of average height but slender and his short, cropped light brown hair hung loosely about as he glanced around while waiting at the foot of the steps. Rick smiled and told his stepsister where he was going. She shrugged in response, and he bolted out the door, closing it behind him. He got his bike from the back porch and met his friend. They rode their bikes to the bottom of a large red clay dirt hill and inspected it for a good route. The pair had been contemplating seeing how much speed would be required to not only reach the top, but to try and soar to the opposite side of the smaller hill that lay hidden behind the larger.

They gazed up and down the hill a few moments longer while asking each other's opinion, and decided upon a route located on the central portion of the hill. Smiling, they rode up the hill on the opposing side and positioned themselves to attempt the stunt they were planning, since the weather began to warm up. Josh went first and raced toward the targeted area, using his slender legs like spindly pistons that pumped tenaciously, while using gravity to aid in gaining speed. Rick watched tensely as Josh sped up the hill and jumped as he reached the top. Josh flew in the air momentarily then disappeared. After a few anxious moments later, Rick heard his friend's voice yell the word go.

Rick sped down the hill. Being of larger build his legs helped him gain speed, rapidly causing the wind to whistle past his ears in screeching wine. His bike reached the targeted hill and path, rapidly racing toward the apex. As Rick reached the top, he pulled the handlebars a bit too hard and over compensated so that his bike went tires-up and he landed on his back with an audible "Oof" that left him breathless. The fall did not injure him, however, and he slowly began to rise as he regained his breath. Josh had seen his friend's fall and he ran toward him with worry, but upon observing Rick getting up on his own, his worry began to subside.

"What happened?" asked Josh as he ran the last few steps to his friend's side. The boys were in the valley between the two red clay dirt hills and pondering on the success, and failure, of the jump. Rick finished dusting himself off and walked over to pick up his bike. He looked at the hill he attempted to jump and looked over at Josh with a crooked smile on his face and shrugged.

"I pulled a little too hard," Rick said as he walked with a slight limp and pushing his bike toward his friend. He shook his head and laughed a bit, and Josh smiled in reply and ran to retrieve his bicycle on the other side of the second hill. After the jump was completed, the boys had previously measured about twenty-five yards to a barbed wire fence that kept cows in their field. Because of the barrier and potential speed of travel, you would have to either slow down or bail out before hitting the sharp and electrified wire. The duo was aware of this before it was attempted and had adjusted accordingly.

It was about five or six in the evening and Rick could hear his mother's shrill voice in the distance calling him in for dinner. He bid farewell to his friend, and they agreed to meet at the trailer park pool in the morning. Rick and Josh jumped on their respective bicycles and began their journeys toward their homes. Rick was the first to arrive at his destination because of the short distance from the hill. He rode hard toward his house and returned his bike to its place on the back porch and chained it. He walked around to the front door and went inside, removing his shoes once through the door. Rick's mother was opening Little Caesars' pizza boxes and pouring RC cola into red ROLO cups while mumbling silently to herself. Rick noted this and took his shoes to his room and washed his hands for dinner. He went and sat at the kitchen table with his stepsister and quickly ate his dinner and took a shower in preparation for the coming chocolate chip cookies he smelled in the oven. A dozen of the golden and chocolatey laden sweetness lay in display on a plate and a few were slightly opened due to their size. Within the opened contents oozed the sugared sweetness slightly that enticed the viewer to attempt to steal one warm prize on the circular porcelain exhibit from the female warden. However, Rick waited for his mother to turn her back and he quickly snaked one from the plate and engulfed it before she turned back around.

"Did you just get one of those?" his mother asked, staring at him with a slight glare.

"No. Not at all," Rick mumbled with a full mouth. She scolded him to wait for everyone and he nodded his ascent and went to his room. There, he would stay to avoid his mother and stepfather for the remainder of the night. He had a half bathroom in his bedroom, and he would have no reason to interact with anyone else in the household. Both adults had to work the next day, and Rick and his stepsister would be at home. She would probably have one of her boyfriends over during this time. He never ratted her out and she sort of covered for him. Both stepbrother and stepsister endured the consistent bickering of the adults and would retire to their rooms and simply stay there. Rick stayed awake until around midnight watching television, until he finally fell asleep in exhaustion as the day's events took their toll.

The next morning, Rick woke up upon hearing his stepfather stomp through the small hallway into the bathroom, then, after a few moments, out the door with a slam. He would wait until he heard the car start before getting out of bed to make himself a bowl of cereal and watch television while he ate. After finishing, he rinsed his bowl and placed it in the dishwasher before returning to his room to get ready and complete his weekly chores of mowing the lawn. Rick would take his time; however, it would take him twice the time it should complete. He finished before eleven this day. He went back inside and put on his swimming clothes before eating lunch and leaving the tan trailer.

The pool was rectangular in shape and made of concrete with an area with umbrellas and tables to eat snacks or get out of the sun for a bit. The building was a long structure with long windows that spanned the length so the owners could view the swimmers. On the inside sat various pool tables in the southern portion and ten feet from the aluminum screen door entry. A green carpet adorned the floor that was moderately splattered with chili or various other foods and drink stains. Tables were placed beside the windows with four hard plastic blue chairs sat in pairs on either side with the service desk opposite the windowed wall, and on the far side was the entrance to the swimming pool and the remains of a go-kart track.

Rick walked up to the counter and paid the one-dollar admission to the pool. He walked outside and picked an open chair to put his towel and drink. There were only three other people sharing the pool with him currently. A lady and her child were playing in the shallow end of the pool, and two teenage girls lay in a couple of corner chairs soaking in the morning rays. He walked over and dipped a toe into the deep end to check its temperature. Its cold water sent a slight shiver up his spine, and he quickly jumped into the cooler water to reduce the shock. He swam around for a few moments until he heard a call from the pool entry. Rick turned his head and found his friend, Josh, waving while walking toward Rick. He returned the wave with a smile and swam toward the side and talked to his friend without shouting.

"How are you feeling this morning? You ate it pretty hard yesterday," said Josh with a mocking grin.

'Oh, I'm fine. I'm ready to try again later, if you want," Rick asked half-heartedly. He truly did not want to replay yesterday's failure. The fall had not truly hurt but had knocked the breath from him. There were a lot of rocks around the newly formed dirt hills, and he very nearly hit his head on one.

"Nah, remember we're all playing hide and seek tonight. I believe everyone in the neighborhood is coming, ain't they?"

asked Josh while looking at Rick with a pleading look on his face. The other neighborhood boy had a thing for his stepsister and her friends. To be fair, Rick had a thing for a few of her friends and Rick used this to his advantage to gain favor with the older girls. Rick smiled at his friend's question with a devious grin.

"Yes. Tell everyone she's having a couple of her friends over. You know the older kids are going to do their own thing," said Rick with a laugh. He was aware of the summertime teenage hormones that ran rampant among the hot-blooded teenagers.

The two swam around for a while and jumped in and out until finally sitting in their chosen chairs. Metallica's "One" played through the outdoor speakers and an indoor juke box provided a differing atmosphere of head-banging and the scent of coconut tanning oil. The boys laughed and joked while sitting in their chairs and watched as people begin to wander in. The sun had passed the zenith and fell behind graying clouds when Rick noticed the time read two o'clock in the afternoon, and he realized he would have to return home. As Rick got up from his chair and started to dry off, he noticed a darkly-tanned overweight man walk through the entry gate. He had never seen this newcomer and Rick played all over this neighborhood. He quickly averted his gaze and returned to his task while telling his friend goodbye, putting his shoes on, and headed back to his house. As Rick opened the gated exit to the pool, he noticed his stepsister's boyfriend get in his car and leave. Rick waved at him as the dark green Lumina drove past and his wave was returned. He liked Jeff. Jeff would play pickup basketball games at Rick's and sometimes bring other older teenage boys to play. Their games would last until the streetlights came on and they would have to end their games.

Rick arrived at the front door and went in. He went to his room and retrieved the clothes he would change in to after his shower. After these tasks were complete, he ate a quick snack and went into his room, shut the door, and watched television until he fell asleep. He was drained from the time in the sun and swimming all day and slept until he heard his mother call for dinner. They had made hot dogs and several of his stepsister's friends were circled around the patio table consuming their food and laughing at whatever it was that made the teenage girls giggle. Rick partially ignored the group and went to retrieve a couple of hot dogs and return inside. He fixed two and quickly ate them down, all the while thinking of the hill jump the previous day. The consist chatter of the female group outside began to grate on his nerves and he told his mother he was going outside and ride his bike. He walked around and retrieved his bicycle and coasted down the hill toward the two large red clay dirt hills he and Josh wanted to conquer. As he rode on, Rick spied a black sedan with darkened windows pulling up to the furthest house from the trailer park. This was weird to Rick, for he knew the inhabitants of that residence, and neither of them was home. Rick continued his coast while keeping a lingering eye on the odd vehicle. He noticed the brake lights flash indicating the car being put into park and the driver side door opened. Rick brought his bike to a stop at the bottom of the red clay dirt hill and hid behind a newly growing bush. From his vantage point, he spied the darkly-tanned man from earlier at the pool. The overweight guy walked past the house toward the barn seated behind it and in the field on the opposite side of the fence. He had dark hair and earthy colored clothes that appeared in fashion and in good quality that spoke of wealth. Rick watched until the man disappeared toward the old barn.

Rick began inspecting the hill to see if he could potentially make a successful jump with another try. With dismay, he viewed newly growing foliage beginning to sprout in response to all the rain that has been soaking the region these last few days in brief summer showers. Another appeared to be forming in the east, and the winds were blowing it westward. Rick's father and grandfather had served in the Army and had taught him a little of navigation and weather pattern recognition. He noted with the coolness and speed of the blowing wind, another brief storm would quickly blow through and thoroughly wet everything. The blowing wind brought another sensation to his senses as well. It was the sickly-sweet smell of death and decay. He thought that an animal was dead in the vicinity, and he was going to try and locate its source before jumping on his bike and returning home before the storm hit. Rick noticed the smell grew stronger as he rounded the first red clay hill, and was directly to the side of the second. He came to the other side of the second hill and continued moving while scanning the ground in search of the hidden carcass. Suddenly, to his left, there came a banging sound of large doors slamming shut and the smell began to curiously dissipate. Rick wondered at this momentarily and was shaken from his revelry by a loud thunder crack that sent him racing toward his bike. While he was bent over picking up his red and black mode of transportation, he observed the black car leaving the trailer park and traveling toward the main highway. The boy shrugged and hopped on his bike to make his way home just as the rain began to lightly fall.

The storm lasted for quite a bit longer than a summer shower. Thunder roared and wind shook the single-wide trailer that housed the family and hosted five other teenage girls. The storm had effectively ruined their plans for the nighttime game, so the girls resigned to rent and watch movies while irritating Rick, until he locked his bedroom door and went to sleep. He could still hear them cackling through the night until the thunder began to drown them out and he drifted to sleep.

The next few days went much the same, and oddly enough the stranger made many more sudden appearances. Each time he would arrive, it would be to enter the pool after noon, and he would be spotted later that day parked at the house at the end of the trailer park. Rick had continued to smell the slight smell of death at times. Eventually, he would bring this to Josh's attention and ask him to help him investigate.

He would not today though, and instead slowly ride his bicycle around the trailer park alone. Rick was going to his father's for a couple of weeks in a couple of days, which he was both happy and grateful for. He did not feel like he could be himself here and was more a houseguest than a family member within his mother's household. He smiled at the knowledge he was going to be with his father for an extended period. The pair always had fun together and enjoyed one another's company.

Rick's mind lingered on that thought while simultaneously enjoying the feeling of the warm air that gently caressed his face in the kisses of youthful happiness. A happiness and joy that is found in those that have yet to discover the existence of time and its passage. Rick's slow pace comforted him and allowed Rick to enjoy the scenery and the overall pleasantness of the day. He continued to follow the road around to the left side of the swimming pool in front of his mom's trailer and on the opposite side of the swimming pool entrance. He followed the path until it connected with the old kart track. As he began to turn his wheel right toward the tracks beginning, he observed that same fat, dark-haired, and tanned man drove up in the black car and parked in the same driveway as always.

This time Rick could view where the man would go and give him a place to look for clues that his inquisitive mind craved. Rick stopped his bike and watched intently as the car door began to open, and he quickly lay flat on the ground and watched. As always, the man got out of his car, scanned the area, shut his door, and then began walking behind the house. This time Rick observed as the man walked up to the barn and unlocked the large doors then proceeded inside. The doors slammed behind him and there would be no sign of him for many moments. This time it was more in the realm of four hours, and the sun was beginning to set behind the western horizon before the barn doors swung open and the man lumbered out and walked toward his car. He stopped at his car door and quickly scanned the surrounding area while getting the correct key placed between his right index finger and thumb, then opened the car door. He gave one final glance, then sat in the driver's seat and shut the door. Rick lies still for many more moments before he finally heard the car start and observed the taillights turn on. He watched the car traverse the road and headed toward the highway before rising to finally investigate where the strange man went each night at dusk.

Rick rode his bike down the grass hill on the opposite side of the racetrack and past the last house toward the large brown barn. The sun was still peaking over the trees in a sliver of light, as if it wanted to hide its eyes from what was going to be observed by the youth. The wind began to whistle through the stand of pines that flanked the barn and cooled the summer warmth on his sweat-spotted clothes. The blowing wind brought another odd characteristic that instilled that quiver of fear that chilled Rick on this summer evening: the smell of death. The smell grew stronger as Rick approached the barn. As he observed the doors, he brought his left forearm to shield his nose from the smell. Rick's fear began to send his imagination into overdrive, and his eyes widened to try and observe anything that could possibly move. The wind blew the doors to the barn slightly ajar and loosened the "Dummy" locked portals to allow the western setting rays to slither eastward through the other side. Rick was ten feet from the door now and he began to sweat and his hands began to shake with greater intensity. He squinted hard to view the contents of the barn from his vantage point of only three feet away. The smell was much stronger now, and his hand unconsciously found the chain that linked the doors together. Rick, still covering his nose, peered inside and noticed that a path that could be driven through if needed bisected the barn. Five stalls with individual doors sat on either side of the path, which had another smaller path that rounded to the left at the other end of the barn. The "A" framed structure appeared to have the capability of storing a numerous number of items, which increased the inquisitive stirrings and relinquished some of his fear. He did not want to be caught, so he did not bring a flashlight. He did not think one would be necessary for this evening's scouting event.

The sun's rays began to sink further behind the western tree line, as if to rest from the tiring events of today. Rick found a ladder that he thought would lead to a better view on the left side between the second and third stalls. Between the planks of lumber, he thought he saw something swinging on the opposite side, close to the wall, and the smell of decay was still strong, slightly upsetting his stomach. He climbed over several hay bales, careful not to knock over or disturb anything. When he reached the apex of the mound of hay bales, Rick peeked his head over the hay to view the sights below. What he saw at that moment scared him and caused him to fall backwards and tumbled over the bales of hay to land against the railing on the ladder. Rick quickly scrambled down the ladder and began running toward the barn entrance and glanced to his right as he ran. He saw the swinging black wrapped things on the hooks and flashlights in the distance. Rick bolted through the barn doors and ran his bike down the hill until he jumped on its seat and sped to his house. As he quickly locked up his bike, his mind reeled, "How am I going to tell that there are dead bodies hanging in that barn?"

The next morning, Rick began his vacation with his father and would not return to his mother's for a few weeks, thankfully. After his visit was through and he returned to his mother's in the trailer park, he and Josh reconvened to report their findings. After both boys reported, they were still astounded by the wail of police sirens and blue lights that had surrounded the barn and the house on the hill above it. Apparently, the smell of death was that of a guard dog that had hung itself on its chain inside the barn. The dog, it was later reported, was guarding several hundred pounds of marijuana, which the DEA and local police confiscated and arrested the perpetrators. That feeling of fear still lingered with Rick, however, and he still saw the swinging bodies on the hooks.

"Eyes that Look Back"

Chapter 1

DREAMS are a series of thoughts, images, or sensations occurring in a person's mind while asleep. Often, we imagine ourselves in amazing situations, both good and bad, during those restful hours to some varying degree. It is my belief that our goals, accomplishments, and obstacles manifest themselves in ways that inspire joyous or shadowed actions in our realities. Can we bring material things from our dreams and make them real? We often hear about people living their dreams and forcing these astonishing things into reality. Doesn't that also beg the question of, "Can you bring a nightmare into reality?" Such was the howling and puzzling recurring dream from my youth, or was it a nightmare? It remains a puzzle to me with my extended collegiate studies that I have yet to solve. Does the dream or nightmare occasionally enter our reality and plague our waking hours? Do they affect our natural realities and those of our imagination? I have heard it said that if you die in a dream, you die in the natural world as well. Does this mean you can have other experiences that also replay within the natural world? I lay wrapped in my white jacket, and in my white room and laugh maniacally at the silliness of the sun while I ponder those sky-blue eyes.

It was another long day at Lake Shore hospital in the summer for nurse Christine Campbell. After earning her nursing degree from Walter State, the recent graduate was feeling nervous as she embarked on her first job. She had heard the stories of the type of patients that made residence here, and it intrigued her. She always enjoyed the psych aspect of the job and was contemplating continuing to get her grad degree and becoming an APRN, or advanced practice nurse. Christine had family that was prone to mental illness, and she felt obligated to learn how to help them as much as possible. During her musings, she arrived at her last patient's door; that was her only patient in solitary. She remembered in the turnover report this morning that this patient was prone to aggressive behavior and to ensure an orderly was nearby. Christine saw Brandon, an orderly with many years' experience, walking expeditiously down the hallway to meet the new nurse.

"Would you like a standby?" he asked, while nodding toward the last room on the left.

Brandon was a sturdy young man, with broad shoulders and well-muscled arms. He was a gentle person, but he could intimidate others when riled. Christine saw him slam an extremely aggressive patient because they were attacking another patient that was twice Brandon's size. She nodded in assent and finished gathering her meds and paperwork before turning to open the door. Brandon stepped in and opened the door for her and entered the dimly lit padded room to make sure it was safe for her to enter. The room was an eight-by-eight room with a toilet, sink, and bed. A window on the eastern wall gave plenty of sunlight for the patient to view and hear the birds sing.

The staff tied the patient in his jacket and secured him to the bed because of the last evening's events. He had experienced some psychotic episode around two in the morning and had to be bound for his safety. He was ranting and screaming about bright blue wolf's eyes staring at him and then went suddenly silent for about thirty minutes. After that time passed, he began throwing himself at the door, raving about some wolf in his cell with him, and he was trying to escape it. Many milliliters of drugs later, he was bound and laid as comfortably as possible on his bed in solitary.

"Good morning Mr. Humphries. Did you rest okay?" Christine asked in a cheerful voice and demeanor.

The patient rolled his eyes slightly toward the nurse's voice and allowed a steady stream of drool to escape the right side of his mouth. Christine mentally berated herself but continued to smile at the unfortunate man before her, trying to be reassuring.

"Here are your medications, Mr. Humphries. I mixed them with some applesauce to make it easier on you. Is that okay?" The patient slightly nodded, and she carefully spooned the meds in his mouth and observed him swallow it down. She smiled at him and performed her morning assessment, took his vital signs, and ensured his comfort before turning and leaving the room with Brandon behind her, closing the door.

Christine observed the patient through the window in the door for a moment and walked over to her cart to complete her rounds.

"That poor man seems heavily drugged. I wonder what his actual diagnosis is and what flipped the switch? I'll have to see if I can sit in on the doctors' meeting for that one," she said to herself while completing her scheduled medication passes to her patients that were seated in the common room.

Christine made small talk with these patients. They were toward the end of their treatment or well enough to be around everyone, including staff and other patients. She eventually made it back to a desk and began charting her findings for her first rounds and med passes on her patients and went back to Mr. Humphries' room on the far-left corner of the eastern wing. She walked down the hallway, pondering what his full story could be. They diagnosed him with paranoid schizophrenia, with paranoid delusions and aggressive behavior, but that was his diagnosis, not the cause. Of course, it was a neuro-imbalance of some sort, but that was not his story, and she was curious. She crept up to the window in his door and peered inside the room, her arms wrapped around her midriff to help quell her nervousness. He lay where she left him about an hour ago, trussed in his straight jacket and chained to a bracket that lay within the wall on the other side of the bed. She noticed his tousled brown hair and heard him moan. He looked towards the only window in his room and gave a grotesque smile to a red-bellied robin perched outside. It was a weird drug-induced sort of smile that looked like a drunken clown that spewed rivers of spittle from his mouth. Christine sighed and shook her head. It would be days before the doctors made their rounds. She hoped she worked on those days so she may glean some insight into this mysterious and dangerous patient. As she turned to leave, Mr. Humphries wailed at something in the room. Quickly, Christine spun around and hurriedly scanned the room for anything that may have triggered the poor man. On the northern wall opposite the door, she could have sworn she saw a shadow dart toward her anxious patient. Christine stepped in front of the door to get a clear view of the room and saw nothing but her quivering patient. Other than being frightened, he seemed okay, so she walked back to her cart to check the doctor's orders for potential anti-anxiety medications for him.

"That was a clear shadow that darted across that man's room. I saw that! I wonder what that could have been? I guess it could have been a cat, but on the fourth floor? That seems highly unlikely. I will get Brandon to accompany me and search the room a bit after I get him calmed down," thought Christine as she sat down at her cart and began scanning the orders and medication lists.

Unable to find anything suitable, she asked Brandon to join her in checking on Mr. Humphries if he had time. He agreed, and both Christine and Brandon took turns keeping an extra eye on their most mysterious patient. The remainder of the twelve-hour shift was uneventful for Christine and Brandon. After a few hours of the shadow incident, Mr. Humphries settled back into his bed and resumed grinning at the random birds that alighted on his window and occasionally cackled in drug-induced delight. Christine gave and finished her report to the night shift nurse, Paul, and went to the locker room to retrieve her personal items and go home for the evening. Unlike some nurses that could leave their work at work when they were off, Christine could not. She had to research and find the answers to the questions in her head. While leaving, she took a moment to review her event calendar and saw that she had arranged a night out with the girls. Her research would have to wait this evening. Tonight, she would enjoy herself and start tomorrow with a clear head. Well, clear-ish. She smiles to herself in acknowledgement of her scheduled drunken evening escapades with a group of girls that had low inhibitions. As she approached her car, she decided that work would be here tomorrow, but tonight would be fun. She got in her car, giddy with expectations, and sped to her house to get ready for her night out.

Paul was reading over Christine's notes as he observed her get onto the elevator to go to her car. He shook his head with a smile from ear-to-ear as he looked over the nursing notes. They were a bit too detailed, but that will lessen, as she gets older in the nursing profession. Paul was an average-sized middle-aged man with graying hair and wore glasses. He was a mild-mannered man and did not upset easily, which made him an ideal caregiver for the hospital's current population. After perusing the notes a second time, he double counted his med cart and began his rounds. He heard the rumors of the strange occurrences that had followed their most recent admission. Paul had overheard how Mr. Humphries had screamed and belligerently wailed about a wolf inside his cell, then began throwing himself against the door to escape. This type of action happened often in this unit, so he overlooked most of what they said.

He continued walking the white-walled and white-tiled hallway toward the end of the west wing. Paul was about half-finished with his med passes and assessments and was eager to begin his charting with hopes of an easy shift when he noticed movement from his outer peripheral vision on his right side. It was a brown streak that zoomed past him and kept to the outer recesses of his vision, completely preventing any identifying view of the thing. Still, the vision had him a bit shaken, so he took to visibly searching the empty rooms for any sign of anything that resembled the streaking hallucination. After several minutes of active searching, Paul shrugged his shoulders and laughed nervously, then continued his rounds.

The search had put him about twenty minutes behind, however, which made Paul rush through his assessments and med passes to finish in a timely and safe manner. Finally, he arrived at Mr. Humphries' room at the end of the eastern wing. Paul looked down the hallway and saw Sarah half-jogging toward his location. Sarah was a shorter and stockier female of African descent. She kept her hair in tight braids and coiled in a small bun on the back of her head. She was a sweet woman with a calming disposition, except in public. Sarah loved to let loose outside of work. Of course, in this business, everyone has some sort of release to keep a reign on his or her personal sanity.

"Are you ready, Mr. Paul? Christine said this one had quite the day and night. She said that he was hallucinating pretty hard and had to be drugged," said Sarah with a worried look on her face.

She had a firm belief in ghosts and the haunting tales that surrounded this hospital. Sarah had claimed she saw ethereal apparitions and shadows on various floors and units throughout the hospital. She worked at this facility for about eight years and had seen a few inexplicable things.

"Yes, ma'am. They kept him medicated for most of the day and the doctors want him to have a decent night's rest this evening. I hope they help the poor man find some peace after their interview. I heard they must wait until Dr. Metcalf returns from his vacation next week. He won't know what world he's in by that point." Paul frowned at this statement.

He did not believe in drugging a patient beyond thought and calling them healed or better. Paul looked through the door window and saw his patient staring at the window with a wild-eyed stare that seemed to be fixated on something outside. Mr. Humphries kept staring out the window as Paul and Sarah entered the room cautiously.

"Good evening Mr. Humphries, I'm Paul, your nurse for this evening and this is your aide, Sarah. We must take your vital signs and do a quick assessment, okay? Before we go through all that, we are going to give you your scheduled medications. Would you like us to loosen that jacket and allow you to do this or do we need to leave it on?" Paul asked the patient while Sarah stared at the nurse in disbelief and mild shock.

Paul reached over Mr. Humphries and loosened the chain that bound the straight jacket while maintaining a firm grip on the chain to keep some control. Sarah stood by and to Paul's left to allow herself the angle that provided the clearest trajectory if she had to tackle the patient. Paul helped Mr. Humphries up from his laying position to a seated position and loosened the straps that bound the patient's arms to his sides. While diligently working to give his patient a reprieve, he did not notice the vague look leaving his patient's face and being replaced by a calculating look. Sarah tensed in response, as she was aware of the intense attention Mr. Humphries gave Paul, then he shifted his gaze to meet hers. This action startled Sarah out of her intended action, and as soon as Paul released the last strap that bound his patient's arms, Mr. Humphries acted. He knocked Paul to the side with his left elbow and grabbed Sarah's shirt with his right hand that was propelled by a powerful lunge. Humphries threw her on top of Paul, preventing them from giving immediate chase as he sprang toward the door. The pair struggled for a few moments as they watched helplessly as their patient ran out of the room.

No sooner did Mr. Humphries grab the right side of the doorframe to slingshot himself down the eastern corridor did the pair hear the yelp of a canine and their patient fall backward halfway through the door. The pair could not reach him in time to prevent the tell-tale thunk of Mr. Humphries' head hitting the tile hospital floor. The caregivers checked C-Spine and for concussion by checking the pupils. Noting the reactivity of his eyes, they maintained his head position and gently laid him in bed and replaced his restraints. Paul gave his drugs through intramuscular injection and he and Sarah left the room, shaken by the event. As the two walked back toward the nursing station from the easternmost portion of the east wing, they both chatted nervously about hearing the clear yelp of a dog. They both checked the entire unit several times throughout their hourly rounds that evening, but found nothing. Shrugging off the event as another rough night, the pair gave their respective reports to the oncoming shift the following morning and slept the night's events away.

Christine's head throbbed through the morning report from Paul. She faintly remembered his account of the unusual yelping noise and Mr. Humphries' aggressive behavior. The recovering nurse was acutely aware that she smelled faintly of alcohol that was emanating from her pores as she sweated. She hoped that the nurse's habitual use of hand sanitizer would mask the smell enough for last night's fun to wear off fully. However, she was sober and, aside from her sleepiness, she could function enough to handle the job capably. So long as she had Brandon on this shift to aid her. She choked down eight hundred milligrams of ibuprofen and washed it down with coffee from the nurse's lounge. Then, taking her med cart and patient notes, she began her rounds. Since she had the same patients as the previous day, she assumed that this morning and afternoon would be easier compared to her last shift. She heard an odd laughter coming from the end of the hall after attending her fifth patient. Before searching the hall, she made a quick stop by the nurse's station to check the staff roster. To her dismay, she discovered Brandon had called off, and the supervisor assigned her the orderly duties as well. Frowning, she frustratingly turned from the nurse's station and went to investigate the source of the screeching hilarity. As Christine feared the noise was coming from the solitary room at the end of the hall, she unconsciously slowed her steps to a more silent and cautious pace. With agonizing slowness, she finally closed the distance to the doorframe of Mr. Active 2: The source of the screeching hilarity was Humphries' room, but when Christine grew fearful, it halted, and screams along with the sound of straining chains replaced it. Christine ran toward the nurse's station and found her charge nurse sitting behind the desk making phone calls. The supervisor noted the junior nurse's expedited approach and calmly rose to meet her. Christine began explaining the situation to the charge nurse as they walked toward Mr. Humphries' room. The charge nurse reached into her pocket and pulled out a syringe full of Benadryl, Phenergan, and Ativan to mix the combination with saline to inject the aggressive patient.

As both nurses reached the door, the noises stopped after an audibly strong yank on the chain, followed by a thud on the floor. When the pair reached the front of the door, the sight they beheld astounded them. The man had ripped his left hand from his restraints and was all akimbo on the floor and upside down. As the two inspected their patient, they found light colored brown hair tightly gripped between his fingers. Puzzled, the two nurses began inspecting his head for any wounds or abrasions, especially from the high probability of him pulling his hair from his head. They put the restraints back in place and tightened them more securely to ensure the patient's safety, and gave him the prepared cocktail of drugs. Next, they retrieved the hair from his grasp and sent the hairs to the lab to find out their source and continued their day.

Shaken from her earlier stupor, Christine finished the remaining shift smoothly, other than being short staffed. She would tell Brandon what was on her mind the next time they worked together, but this was her short week, and this was her last day until the following week. Before she finished giving Paul the end of shift report, the lab from downstairs called to report their findings. The odd thing was that they thought bringing the family dog's hair in for a lab specimen was a hilarious joke and hung up the phone with a harrumph. Christine gave the phone an odd look, shook her head, and finished her report to Paul. It would not be until that evening that the laboratory had called and gave Paul the report about a German shepherd's hair follicle test. What was more puzzling, and intriguing, was where did Mr. Humphries find a dog on the fourth floor of a building and in a locked, confined cell? She was developing a sense of unease about returning to work next week. Christine dreaded this most, especially if she had Mr. Humphries as a patient again for another twelve hours. She truly pitied the poor disturbed soul, but something about him gave her the shivers. The new nurse would request another assignment if needed, but she would prefer to not go near that man again. She remained curious and would have to remember to sit in on that interview with Dr. Metcalf.

Paul received his report in the same good-natured manner as always, but his mind reeled at the news of the hair follicle test. He and Sarah had looked everywhere for the dog they heard the night before but could find no trace of the thing.

"What's going on in this hospital? I have heard some strange rumors that were connected to this place, but I have never heard of a haunting that centered on one person here. Why am I thinking about haunting? I've been around Sarah too long." Paul continued his inward conversation while he prepared for the coming trials of the day.

Sarah was off tonight, and he had a new and freshly trained aide this evening. Paul had his reservations, but at least he would not have the entire workload on himself like Christine had earlier. Unlike last night, he was determined to start his round with Mr. Humphries. He traversed the length of the corridor in the eastern wing, eventually reaching the leftmost door where he looked inside Mr. Humphries' room. The patient lay there in his trussed and wrapped state, in a drugged stupor and apparently resting peacefully. He confidently opened the door and did his assessment and took Mr. Humphries' vital signs before giving him his IM injection meds. Paul observed his patient intently, hoping to detect any signs of a reaction, but the patient remained motionless, calmly resting. The older nurse expressed his agreement by nodding and offering a small smile, then departed the room, closing the door as he left. Paul was relieved by this interaction, and the rest of his rounds went smoothly. Upon completing his last medication pass, he sat at the nurse's station to do his charting and nurse's notes. Following approximately one-and-a-half hours, he got up to attend to his patients and provide any needed medication or wound care. Everyone was calm, and this comforted Paul even more. He shrugged away his worry about the potential haunting with a nervous laugh and he began turning out the lights, signifying bedtime.

Hours passed for the weary healthcare workers at a snail's pace. Seconds crept into agonizing minutes, then into painful hours until the hour struck two in the morning. In the deathly quiet eastern corridor arose a slight, at first, wailing howl. Paul was in the restroom as it started, and he did not catch it until he exited. Slowly, the wail increased in volume until Paul heard it keenly, and so did the other patients. Call lights began ringing in response to the howling and some of the sicker patients began howling in response, adding to the cacophony of screeching noise that rose in waves. Paul ran down the hallway of the eastern corridor to locate the source of the entire ruckus when he arrived at Mr. Humphries' room. He looked in the room and saw his patient still trussed up but balled into a quivering state and at the furthest corner of his bed. He walked cautiously into the room, all the while staring at his potentially volatile patient. As he neared the patient, Paul noticed a small splatter of blood dripping down the far corner of the bed where Mr. Humphries was located.

"Mr. Humphries. Mr. Humphries, it's Paul, your nurse. Sir, are you hurt? It looks like you're bleeding," said Paul, edging closer and toward an advantageous position to view the wound. "Sir, I need to look at your arm. It looks like you have hurt it somehow."

Paul reached out and grasped the left arm and gently pulled to remove the potentially loose straight jacket. As Paul began moving the arm, he heard his patient cry in obvious grief, and for the first time, Paul looked in Mr. Humphries' eyes. He did not see the vague, clueless look. He saw clear thoughts of honest fear and sorrow.

"Please. Please, make it go away. It's been tormenting me for so long." Mr. Humphries began crying uncontrollably, and Paul stared in amazement at how tightly bound he remained but was bleeding from his left forearm. Paul left the room to retrieve wound care items from his cart and call Charles, the new orderly, over to assist him. The pair released the patient from the restraints and looked at the obvious puncture wounds to his left arm. After cleaning the wounds and calling the doctor, they returned the patient to his restraints and made him as comfortable as possible before leaving the room. Paul instructed his aide to sit with Mr. Humphries and he would take over his duties until the end of the shift and notified security of a potential wild animal within the building. Paul hoped and prayed that Dr. Metcalf would get back soon. This case was getting too weird, even for him. After Paul gave his shift report that morning, he put in for a three-week, long overdue, vacation. He hoped this was just a hallucination of being overworked, but that was an obvious dog bite. Paul wondered if Mr. Humphries was truly hallucinating, or simply seeing something that was invisible to everyone else but just as real.

As the morning shift report calmed down, the charge nurse received orders from Mr. Humphries' doctor to leave him on a one-on-one watch until his interview. After this action, the patients calmed down by themselves, and the staff reported no more sounds or sightings of a wayward hound. Mr. Humphries got the best sleep in his forty years of life. He began to slowly and intellectually converse with his nurses and aides to the point of bewilderment for those that spoke with him. His caregivers even wondered why he was in solitary and discounted the bizarre reports that surrounded him. They would wonder about other intriguing and disturbing information about this man upon Dr. Metcalf's arrival.

Chapter 2

IT had been three weeks since Dr. Stanley Greene had been an intern for Dr. Metcalf. He received only three days of internship before Dr. Metcalf left for vacation, and Stanley had to wait on Dr. Metcalf's return before resuming his internship. He was required to have two years internship before he could begin his residency and start making money. Currently, when broken down to hour for hour, he was barely clearing minimum wage, and they sent most of his earnings to student loans. Getting this internship was the start of completing his goals, so he shrugged the monetary issues off as a minor inconvenience. He genuinely loved this profession and had an uncharacteristically caring view of his patients. His fellow interns had scolded for this him because they had to remain aim and could not get emotionally close to their patients. In their view, showing feelings of empathy would prevent them from giving quality care to their patients. It was the nurse's job to perform the caring, hand-holding, and hugging nonsense that took too much time away from more concerning matters and sicker patients. Stanley discounted these comments as well. He was the youngest of the accepted interns this year and, being a graduate from Vanderbilt University, medical and psychiatric program at twenty-one, made him highly recruited. He still had his youthful hope of changing the world and inspiring the masses, which consistently annoyed his attendees.

Dr. Greene sat in Dr. Metcalf's office, frustratingly awaiting his mentor that was running two hours late. Tardiness was a pet peeve of Stanley's. He enjoyed a tight and well-rounded schedule that provided him with a continuance of routine that made it easier for him to track other interests. However, Dr. Metcalf was flighty, yet brilliant, so the wait should be worth it. The other thing that frustrated Stanley was the fact that they were here to interview an extremely sick patient today. That poor man had been here for almost three weeks and was just now getting interviewed by his doctors, which further angered him. He could understand if a patient was stable, but to leave one in such an obvious panicked state truly infuriated him. His anger management classes came to mind as Stanley performed deep breathing exercises to calm him.

Another hour had passed, and Dr. Metcalf's car came into view of his office that Dr. Greene impatiently awaited. It was now noon and lunchtime, so Dr. Greene met Dr. Metcalf in the lobby and had their meeting over lunch to save time. Dr. Greene left the office and traversed the second-floor office space toward the stairwell. He turned the latch to open the door and proceeded through. He quickly bounded down the concrete stairwell and calmly exited through the door that led to the lobby below. The lobby is a large, windowed, circular structure that comprised several lounge chairs and couches that were sky-blue and arranged in various angles to provide panoramic views of the mountains from the hilltop office. Such a spectacular landscape provided differing scenarios throughout the year that changed the mood of the workers and patients with their display of color. Dr Metcalf finally parked his Porsche 911 in its assigned parking spot and admired himself in the rearview mirror before finally opening the door and walking toward the hospital. Dr Greene's foot tapped lightly on the tile floor as his impatience mounted, and he had to make an overly conscious effort to quell the burning urge of anger.

"Well, good morning, Dr. Greene," Dr Metcalf greeted while spinning through the spinning door.

Dr Metcalf's shining demeanor melted away Stanley's anger and frustration as they made the grinning salutation. Dr. Metcalf strolled up to Stanley with a jovial leap to his step. The man must have had a wonderful vacation to be at this place so happy. Or perhaps Mrs. Metcalf had something to do with this boyish spring in the man's step? Whatever the reason behind the man's obvious good mood this morning, this observation would make for a good day.

"Have I kept you waiting long?"

Stanley smiled at Dr Metcalf's greeting. This man did not know Stanley had been in his office waiting for hours and his frustration had mounted to an almost volcanic level. Though the molten frustration had lowered to a simmer from the boil it once was.

Stanley replied, "No, sir, not long. I was going through the nurse's notes of the new admissions we had these last few weeks. I arranged the files by floor and by acuity. We have some sick patients, Doctor. Have you heard the strange report from the fourth floor? I was told the nurses on shift tried to call you to report on their findings, but you were still unavailable. This Sidney Humphries has quite the story to tell, apparently."

Dr. Metcalf waved his right hand in a horizontal slashing motion that cut off any more of Dr. Greene's conversation with patients.

"I don't like to talk shop on an empty stomach. Let me get some lunch down and we can go over this stuff."

His nonchalant attitude infuriated Stanley, and he was constantly reminding himself that this internship was worth it. He nodded his assent, however, and followed Dr. Metcalf to the cafeteria, his arms stacked with patient's files and folders, and chose an empty, secluded table for the pair to work while eating. The cafeteria was serving spaghetti and some chicken concoction that smelled of paprika and garlic. After filling their plates, the doctors walked to their chosen table and sat opposite one another. They talked amicably about the vacation that Dr. Metcalf returned from, and the trajectory of Stanley's potential at this hospital and others he was being recruited by. The enthusiastic conversation melted away Stanley's frustration at Dr. Metcalf's tardiness, and the two conversed livelier. As they laughed and talked, the worries and stresses of their job faded into obscurity. Dr. Metcalf preferred this mindset. It allowed for a more observatory position that allowed for better patient care. At least, according to Dr. Metcalf's perspective.

"Alright Dr. Greene, let us hear about our sick ones. Let us start with the file on Mr. Humphries. I seem to recall you telling me of some strange reports from the nurses," questioned Dr. Metcalf as Dr. Greene produced the required chart. "What are your personal impressions on Mr. Humphries?"

Dr. Greene paused for a few moments while thinking of an answer. The superstitious clout that often lingered within these older facilities was something Dr. Greene was aware of, and he knew that one orderly had a particular infatuation with tales of the supernatural and paranormal. Dr. Greene believed that such people often allowed their minds to stimulate ghostly visions and demonic gestures from beyond the veil of the living that influence their lives. It was such nonsense to him. How could someone with an education allow themselves to be influenced by things that current science can explain or the fact that overwork exhausts their bodies and minds?

"I believe his past has a lot to do with it. He has had a very tumultuous life in his short forty years. His mother left him with his grandparents while he was in his formative years. The father died in the Vietnam War and never had that fatherly influence. His mother remarried some years after, however, to an abusive man apparently. The man beat her to death, if you want to call him that, before taking his own life at the end of a bottle. Before Sidney reached the age of eleven, he had to endure those hardships and eventually sent to the care of the state. We know not much about his foster parents. It was only a few years after being in foster care that one family had him committed. The poor man has been in several hospitals before finally coming to us three weeks ago. After reading through his patient history and current nursing notes, I feel like he is suffering from some very real delusions. It seems like his mind has concocted a being that is very real to him. He keeps screaming out about a wolf-like creature with sky-blue eyes in his room tormenting him. However, after they placed him on a one-on-one watch, these instances became less frequent, and Mr. Humphries is showing signs of vast improvement. If he can continue for a week more, we can transfer him to a less secure facility, allowing him to potentially integrate into a normal life. These latest nursing notes and tales of a dog within the facility are almost laughable. I don't understand why they feel the need to write such drivel in a nurse's note, but I digress."

The doctors' meeting about their patients lasted until thirteen hundred, or one PM, and the two gathered their trays and charts and left the cafeteria to begin their rounds. The two started with the least sick patients on their round list on the third floor. Many of those patients were "Walkie Talkie's", or, people that were sick, but only minimally and had control of their ailment using therapy or light medication therapies. They would discharge most of these patients to home or to a rehabilitation facility for drug and alcohol treatment. Others were borderline personality or bipolar patients that could almost live a productive and safe lifestyle but required regular checkups or safety visits. The rounds on these patients flew by. Only the doctors required a brief conversation with these patients. They engaged in friendly conversations with these people instead of interviewing for a potential crisis. Dr. Metcalf smiled at his intern's discomfiture at the speed of their interviews. He understood Dr. Greene's nervous nature as a new doctor. People were getting "Sue Happy" these days and any medical worker had to cross their T's and dot their I's to avoid a costly malpractice suit. Dr. Metcalf knew those reservations would lighten over time, but they would always remain a constant worry while practicing on some of these patients.

Dr. Metcalf and his intern completed their charting and nursing meetings, then made their way to the elevator to continue to the fourth floor. Dr Greene's hands trembled as they approached the patient he earnestly wanted to see, Mr. Sidney Humphries. It astounded him: the rumors and the veil of tragedy that surrounded this man. He wondered at the cause of this most peculiar manifestation of Sidney's fears. Yet, the other circumstances do not add up either.

"Um, Dr. Metcalf, I was wondering about a bit of information," asked Dr. Greene nervously. "I was wondering if we may interview the caregivers before we interview the patient. I would like to have objective information before comparing the subjective." Dr. Metcalf raised an eyebrow in askance.

He wondered if Stanley had put too much thought into the stories of the wayward wolf that plagued the patient. He silently hoped that this intelligent and promising doctor did not fall victim to such nonsense.

"I think that would be an excellent idea, Dr. Greene! Nurses are around the patient much more than we will ever be and they observe the patients' interactions with their treatments and others," Stanley smiled and slightly blushed at the praising tone his mentor had given him.

The stories he had heard ignited such anticipation in him that he eagerly anticipated this interview. Alas, this floor's patients took much longer than the previous with the patient interviews. This floor contained the highest acuity of sick individuals that live at the hospital. They droned on. Over and over, with almost the same bit with each patient. Dr. Metcalf would infer their mental state of mind, and they would respond by prattling on about stardust, the number of dots in the ceiling, or the slight upward slant of the hallway. Stanley wondered how the nurses and aides could manage a shift without smiling at these oblivious individuals. They completely medicated most of them that they sat at a window staring at nothing while a stream of drool oozes down their chin and smelled faintly of urine. Others laugh at the wall or held conference calls on their shoe. Some of the remaining individuals that were in the common room spoke vigorously with the walls and sporadically laughed at a dancing shadow or stray flicker of light. After what seemed like forever, Dr. Metcalf motioned for him to follow, and the pair approached the nursing station where they were beginning their shift report. Fortunately, the two interviewing doctors had both sets of caregivers here at this moment. Dr. Metcalf approached the shift leader and nursing supervisor about the interview with Mr. Humphries and explained the reasoning for the need for the nurses' impressions that had cared for him before. Both nursing supervisor and shift leader retrieved both oncoming and off-going nurses to meet with the doctors in their lounge per request. Perplexed, the two nurses walked toward the doctor's lounge to report on the things they witnessed and observed regarding Mr. Sidney Humphries. After both nurses explained what they witnessed in every detail, Dr. Metcalf excused them to return to work. Next, Dr. Metcalf and Dr. Greene interviewed the nursing aids and compared their impressions with the nurses'. Every detail was the same with the interviewees. Even the incredible ones that involved the hound. The doctors exchanged glances and vigorously shook their heads before fixating on the charts in front of them. After a moment, they replaced the paperwork within manila folders and left to interview Mr. Humphries. Stanley's heart raced as they finally drew nearer to the one patient he wanted to see.

Drs. Metcalf and Greene walked down the eastern corridor to not rile the other patients that were winding down. Interviewing the nurses and aides that were in direct contact with Mr. Humphries took longer than anticipated, and bedtime was approaching.

Finally, they reached the last remaining door down the eastern corridor to the left and Dr. Metcalf looked into Stanley's eyes and said, "It's going to be okay. Relax and stay relaxed. Are you ready? Go ahead," said Dr. Metcalf as he motioned toward the door.

A thousand thoughts began to tornado within Stanley's mind. They were outrageous questions that were impossibilities and could not plausibly be real. The other caregivers noted their observations. Stanley shook his head as if to clear the cobwebs from his mind. He could not, and would not, believe in ghost stories when he had to figure out the best way to help this severely sick man. Still, the nervousness remained with him, and with a shaking hand, Dr. Greene reached for the door to his most mysterious patient's room.

Chapter 3

DR. Greene and Dr. Metcalf entered the secure room with nervous excitement. Dr. Metcalf held his excitement in check and his experience was clear in his demeanor as they entered the room and approached their trussed and bound patient. Mr. Humphries had been doing better since they had enacted the one-on-one watch. Apparently, the slender, middle-aged man hated being alone. Everyone thought this was because of his past but was not clear on their assessment yet. He was clean and healthy-looking this evening. Sidney had washed and combed his brown hair, creating a neat part that centered on his right eyebrow, giving his hair a soft, brown and feathery lightness. He wore an inviting smile that spoke of a welcoming and calm nature as the two approached the man.

"Good morning, doctors," Sidney said with a smile.

His faintly yellow stained teeth spoke of too much fluoride in his drinking water. This was the case with several individuals during these days. Drinking water from the tap had an overabundance of the compound in order to ensure it remained drinkable after the purifying process. At least, that is what most people believed.

"Morning Mr. Humphries. I am Dr. Metcalf, your admitting doctor, and this is Dr. Greene, your resident intern. I heard you had a bit of a rough start. Can you tell us why?" Dr. Metcalf inquired and tapped Stanley to ensure he was prepared to begin his note taking.

Stanley caught the suggestion and got his pen ready to jot anything down that could aid in their deciphering of this patient.

"Let us begin with your earliest memories and we'll go from there. If there is an event that is uncomfortable for you to discuss, let us know and we will pause and move on. Does that sound okay with you?"

Sidney nodded his head in response to the older man's question, and Dr. Metcalf smiled with approval. He and Dr.

Greene pulled two chairs in front of the brown-haired and bound man to prepare for their interview. Sidney smiled at the pair and was joyous about their visit and easing his debilitating fear of being left alone. After the three were comfortable and seated, Dr. Greene produced a voice recorder to add to his note taking. He did not want to miss any detail that could aid in solving the mystery that was this man.

"Alrighty, Mr. Humphries. Let us start at the beginning," Dr Metcalf said while pressing the record button and preparing his pen and notepad.

After his preparations, Dr. Metcalf and Dr. Greene observed a haunted look that began to swiftly creep over their patient's face, and they promptly prepared themselves in case action was required. They both remembered nurse Paul's account of this slender man overpowering him and his aid and almost escaping the facility.

"Well, sir. My mother entrusted me to my grandparents' care when I was approximately two or three. In those earliest years in the mountains, a place called "Green Corner" on the other side of the river just off the Waterville NC exit and up the mountain, held some of my fondest memories. My earliest memory, however, is when I was about two and the house caught fire. I was in my crib when everyone had gotten out of the place. Eventually, realizing my mother had left me in the inferno, my grandfather raced within to retrieve me. I still remember the heat from the flames that licked the surrounding wood within the house." Mr. Humphries' eyes gained a haunted and distant look about them before he took a breath and continued.

"Some time after that, grandfather purchased a single wide trailer for the family to stay in because of the catastrophe. It was during this time my mother was working for Newport National Bank in Newport, TN. My father was still in Germany at the time in the Army and my mother had elected to keep her and me here within the states to be closer to family. So she said. She would leave me with my grandparents for months on end, with no correspondence of any kind. I found out later she was committing adultery with a man named Etherton while my father was overseas and leaving me with my grandparents. I loved it there.

We had a small farm of animals that included chickens, a hog named Oscar, a couple of dogs, and a vegetable garden that kept us fed all year round. There was no store for miles around and our closest neighbors were the Prices that lived on the opposite side of the mountain. It was peaceful there. I remember chasing the chickens and helping my grandmother in her garden, stacking wood, and repeatedly asking my uncle if he would let me chop. The sadness over the death of Oscar. I loved that hog. I would play with it and feed it lettuce from our garden. My uncle used to tease me about playing with my food, which I never really understood. Until they took Oscar to the slaughterhouse. I remember I cried for days at my uncle's revealing that my grandparents had sent my friend off to die. Then the delivery arrived from the butcher. I remember eating a thick and tasty piece of smoked bacon, then my uncle laughingly pointed out that I was eating my friend. To be honest, I thought Oscar tasted amazing and my uncle never used that jab on me again. I remember asking if I could have another piece of Oscar several times that evening. We had no electricity where my grandparents lived, nor running water other than a small spring creek that ran in its path on the opposite side of the small trailer. We had a wood stove outside that we cooked our meals on, a large metal washbasin that I bathed in, and a kerosene heater for warmth in the winter. Although, a simple and humble lifestyle, I enjoyed my days there immensely. I did, however, continuously ask my grandfather when my mother would return, which he would reply with an "I don't know, son" and continue about the day. I saw only pictures of my father because of his passing in Vietnam years before I was born. I remember my grandmother showing me his pictures and thinking that I had a werewolf for a father. Both my grandparents would tell me stories about his youth and how hardworking and honest my father was. My mother would explain what a lazy low-life he was, and she tried to instill that belief in me, to no avail. Yet, I loved my earliest adventures in the rolling green mountains of nowhere. I lived those days in impoverished ignorance that left me happy in the knowledge I had loved from my grandparents, aunts, and uncle. I saw almost nothing of my mother during those first few years. She would occasionally pick me up and keep me over the weekends. That is when I saw it. During the summer months of my third year, she picked me up from my grandparents on a Friday. I remember she drove a tan Ford escort. That day, she brought me a present. This was customary for her. She would always bring a toy or something of that nature. She spoke with my grandparents for a moment while I put myself in my car seat and played with my new toy. My imagination was fantastic during those times."

Mr. Humphries' gaze drifted to the window as he noticed a brightly colored blue jay that landed on the windowsill outside. It began to chirp and sing, which drew the patient's attention toward it in a rapt wonderment that distracted from his tale. Dr. Greene noted the distraction and looked at Dr. Metcalf in askance. The senior doctor smiled at his intern and subtly shook his head, showing him to say nothing and be patient. After ten minutes of enjoying the loud blue bird, Mr. Humphries turned his attention back to his interviewers and continued as if nothing happened.

"After arriving at the single-wide trailer my mother was renting, I think it was over in Denton. Anyway, the trailer was by a river and the neighbor had horses that were housed in a barn across from mothers. My routine was that when we arrived there, I would go outside and play until it got dark. She would often yell at me to return to my forested home if I ventured inside. This would bother me immensely, as I only aspired to be around her because I missed seeing her during those long absences. However, I had befriended the neighbor's horses and would visit them often. They greeted me at the fence whenever I approached and would allow me to pet them and feed them grass or hay. I named them 'Clompers' and 'Chompers,'" said Mr. Humphries as he rolled his lips back and made smacking noises with his lips and mouth while clopping his fists together, trying to mimic the horses' sounds. Dr. Greene had to turn away to hide the smirk that quickly creased his serious face. He would have to practice a "poker face" for times such as these if he were to appear nonbiased to the situation and accurately diagnose and record the events and conversation taking place.

After the display, Mr. Humphries continued, "After visiting with my large friends, I would venture toward the river and throw rocks at them. They warned me not to risk getting too close to the river for fear of me falling in. My mother said that she never learned to swim and had fears of drowning, so I only got so close. When the lightning bugs flashed, I knew it was time to get back inside. I remember walking through the forested area, with its tall pines, maples, sycamores, and birch trees. To me, they were gigantic. I would often wish I could fly to their tops like the birds. However, the sound of the rushing river always relaxed me as I walked toward my mother's trailer from the river. There was a small deer trail that I always took that was on the western portion of the property she rented. Another trailer sat on a one-acre lot that mirrored the one my mother rented. On the southern side of the property line sat the river, a small creek with a young tree line to the north, an overgrown forested area to the east and the barn with the horses on the west, to give you guys an idea of the layout."

Mr. Humphries' eyes darted toward the door in a startled fashion that resulted in both other men to jump as well. Upon seeing nothing, Dr. Metcalf looked at Dr. Greene and shrugged, then turned to Mr. Humphries and urged him to continue. After a few breaths, the haunted look that had briefly crossed his face relaxed.

Mr. Humphries took a deep breath then continued, "After I would come back inside, my mother and I would wash our hands and have dinner. Sometimes we would watch a movie, but most times I would lie on the couch, eat popcorn, and watch the string of sitcoms that used to invade basic cable those days. While the television was occupied, my mother would perform her cleaning chores.

"One evening, we rented a couple of movies and were watching those while she cleaned. One of them being the Disney cartoon, "Peter Pan" and the other was an accidental rental. The person at the movie rental place had erroneously placed the wrong title in the wrong box. The title of that movie was, "Running with the Devil." I remember when the movie started and read the title that scrolled across the screen. It terrified me so much that I hesitantly drew the blanket over my eyes. The last thing I remember was the sound of a washing machine. Its rhythmic swooshing of water and the rocking bumps of an occasional off-balanced load would put me to sleep. That night is when the dream first began. In the dream, I was being chased by something in the eastern woods. I knew that if I could make it to the horses on the western side, they would help me escape whatever foul evil followed and nipped at my heels. Finally, I broke through the forest line. I noticed that, as I sped across the neighbor's lawn, my steps became lighter, and I began floating between steps. When I reached the halfway point of the yard, I would leave the earthen floor and fly. When my feet were about three to four feet from the ground, I would feel a warm breath and spittle splash across my ankle. I would look back to see a large tan dog stare at me as I flew across the treetops. It would follow me for a while, then turn and head back into the eastern woods. I remember laughing at the thing as I flew across the river and back, never soaring higher than the treetops. I could imagine nothing higher reaching than those behemoths. After what seemed like forever, I would eventually return to my mother's trailer, finding the animal that had hunted me hidden. My hand reached for the doorknob, my eyes would spring open, and it would be Saturday. I remember being confused, laying there in my own bed, when I knew I had fallen asleep in the living room. I would think about how I had arrived in my current state for some moments until concluding that my mother had put me in my pajamas and carried me to bed. I pulled the covers to the side of me and threw my legs over the side of the bed and into a seated position." Mr. Humphries' eyes glazed over as his story took yet another pause.

The haunted look that had faintly invaded his gaze earlier had returned. It had more intensity. Sweat beaded on Mr. Humphries' forehead as he began his recollection. His hands clenched and unclench in obvious anxiety and tension. Dr. Greene and Dr. Metcalf looked at one another and positioned themselves in a safe position to deal with this patient. Dr. Metcalf had a syringe in hand in preparation to administer pharmaceutical restraint if necessary, and Dr. Greene stood nearer the door with another syringe.

Mr. Humphries' eyes darted with increased speed, and he twitched, a motion that was imperceptible. Tension was rising for the doctors. Reports from nurses, both odd and clinical, began filtering through both doctors' minds. Both men edged closer to their respective positions, preparing to do whatever they must ensure their patients' safety. Mr. Humphries' eyes shot to the door where Dr. Greene stood, and he whimpered as a single tear fell from his eye. Noticing this reaction, Dr. Greene turned to follow Mr. Humphries' gaze toward the door just behind him and heard a paw scratching at the door as if an animal were asking for permission to enter. Puzzled, Dr. Greene went to the door and peered outside the door's window. Noticing nothing but while walled and white tiled floor, he shrugged and turned his attention back toward his patient.

During this time, Dr. Metcalf had used the distraction to grab Mr. Humphries and inject the prescribed medication he had for his delusions and waited for them to perform their required action. Dr. Greene and Dr. Metcalf maintained their positions and postures while observing Mr. Humphries' reaction to the medication. Dr. Metcalf injected only a fraction of his prescribed dose so his patient could continue the interview without making him comatose. It took only a few minutes for the drug cocktail to take hold, and Mr. Humphries' demeanor relaxed. After waiting several more moments, Dr. Metcalf instructed Dr. Greene to resume his position and continue scribing his observations.

"Mr. Humphries? Are you feeling better, sir? I injected you with some medicine to help you stay relaxed while discussing this, obviously traumatic, event. Do you need some more time, or can you continue?" inquired Dr. Metcalf, leaning back in his chair to get more comfortable.

It took a few more moments for Mr. Humphries to digest the information with his intoxicated mind, but eventually he nodded in assent and shook his head as if to clear it, then continued.

"My apologies, doctor. I do not know what happened there. In my dream, I remember sitting on the edge of my bed. My head turned to look out my bedroom window to marvel at the morning sun. I remember feeling its warmth and getting eager about the day's exploration. Rising from my seated position, I felt the carpet tickle my toes with its brown softness. My muscles flexed and extended as I stepped toward my bedroom door and reached for the doorknob. I remember looking at my toys and wondered if I wanted to play with them before my mother woke up. The doorknob was cold as I turned it, opening my bedroom door that led to a small hallway. I turned left and went into the bathroom to relieve myself. Not bothering to wash my hands, I left the bathroom, turning right toward the living room and kitchen. My stomach growled, so my young mind made myself a bowl of cereal since my mother was asleep. I viewed the island that separated the kitchen from the living room and the sugar and flower bowls that sat atop it to the right of the kitchen sink. In front of the island sat a dark tan couch that was made of a thin silky fabric that made its way into our home from a yard sale. In front of the couch sat an ovular coffee table that had a glass top with a lower wooden shelf. At the right of the exit of the hallway sat the matching love seat to the couch that stood about a foot beyond the entertainment center that covered an outside window. As I was entering the living room, my right leg bumped into the love seat, causing a slight thumping noise. I gazed down briefly at my leg, and my head returned to its normal position before I saw it. Standing in the middle of our living room, and just beyond the couch, stood a tan German shepherd. It had darker brown fur on its back with white spots that resembled that of a newly born fawn. However, it was mostly light tan and its back stood almost three feet from the ground. When I bumped into the love seat, the sound alerted the animal before. It slowly turned its head in response to the noise almost humanly. My first observation was the drool dripping fangs that sparkled wet in the sun's rays. Their long and yellowed points sent a shiver of fear through my body that I felt acutely. The next was the smile that was splayed across its face. It was a sinister, mocking grin that bespoke of violence. Last, and most memorable, were the eyes. Those sky-blue eyes. Yet, as soon as our eyes met, I fell backward as if pulled from the living room and toward my bed. It felt as if I was gently carried back to my room while lying in a supine position. I saw the animal turn and followed me as I floated. I felt my right foot bump the wall as I turned the corner back into my bedroom while I floated.

It felt as if two invisible arms sat me back on my bed and returning me to the seated position I started in. It was then I noticed the animal's head come into view from my position and it turned it gaze on me. At the moment, its eyes found mine sitting on my bed from the hallway. The door to my bedroom slammed shut, barring the animal from getting in. I felt a warm sensation come over me and I looked down to observe urine in the front of my pants," Mr. Humphries concluded with a chuckle.

His eyes fluttered as the medications took full effect, and Dr. Metcalf nodded to Dr. Greene. They stayed in the room a moment longer and observed their patient. Confident he was resting, they turned and left the patient's room and headed toward the doctors' lounge to discuss their findings. The manifestation of his abandonment issues had deluded his reality to an astounding effect. He ardently believed this tan dog creature hunted him in waking reality as in his dream. Dr. Metcalf and Dr. Greene remained silent as they traveled down the corridor toward the elevator, lost in their own personal thoughts. As they reached the elevator, Dr. Greene thought he heard a faint yelping noise, and with abruptness, turned to peer down the hallway toward Mr. Humphries' room. A shiver ran the course of his bones, and in response he bolted toward the eastern wing, leaving a confused Dr. Metcalf standing at the elevator. Wind and startled looks flew past Dr. Greene as he sprinted the length of the ward toward his destination. When he arrived, the view of Sidney's hung body lying across the foot rail of his bed startled and mortified him. After removing the strangling device and trying to perform CPR, they announced his time of death. Dr. Metcalf and Greene escorted the body to the coroner for autopsy to determine the cause of death. They would later find that Mr. Sidney Humphries had died of a massive heart attack. However, the reasoning behind these findings remained unclear as to the obvious physical health of the patient. Some most astounding discoveries of canine hair being found in his bed linens after his death sent a circulation of rumors around the hospital. Dr. Greene and Metcalf would later relate this patient to other inexperienced doctors in the years to come to scare them into following policy. These rumors had another effect on the nursing staff. Paul, Sarah, and Christine retired and found other jobs. What the trio experienced in that building, coupled with the stories from the doctors, was enough for them to solidify their collective decisions, to find a new line of work.

It Stands in the Middle

Chapter 1

HUMAN action and reaction have varied throughout our existence. We have looked to everything within and without endeavoring to simplify the world that surrounds us to better understand its chaos. We try to answer questions by labeling aspects of life into neat files to cabinet those answers to known questions for later reference. However, some information gets filed incorrectly, resulting in a stream of life's unfortunate lessons that are learned through terrible and sometimes violent means. Here in the present, it happens less often. You do not hear about people starving and going mad from the pain of hunger. People no longer speak of emergent food shortages that leave parents worried for their children that enforce a terrible anxiety and desperate actions. People often question if things like hunger and mental anguish can push an individual over the barrier and fling the violent switch into the one position. Sometimes, people look toward infernal influences to explain the travesties that surround them. Sometimes, it would seem very logical to simplify an answer into that of an infernal category to explain the terrible chaos and evil that surrounds some people. Certain tainted individuals carry a dark veil hanging over them. Determining when a stain or taint appears on someone's soul is questionable. Perhaps the darkened blood has flowed through the veins since the babe pumped its first heartbeat? Perhaps several unfortunate circumstances and hardships cultivated the taint over a period, helping create the shroud of darkness. These contemplations have lasted for thousands of years, to date, and take relevance within a small Appalachian town on the Tennessee North Carolina state border.

Old Man Winter took his time leaving this year. School let out early due to snow and icing roads making delivering the children back to their home a dangerous endeavor. Cars lined the driveway in front of the school in a file behind buses that were anxious about the treacherous trip. Tennessee found itself in mid-April. Just yesterday, we were wearing shorts and looking forward to our spring break when the blizzard hit. It began last night with rain that was blown in from the north and brought the cold with it. Temperatures plummeted and the falling rains turned to ice and snow, which continued to fall today, raising and building walls of white to an astonishing height.

Children waited in the school cafeteria or in the gym for the early dismissal. All the young people were eager to leave the building and return home, or at least anywhere other than the school building. Children that rode the bus sat in the cafeteria and were monitored by two or three of the elementary school teachers. Cosby School is a small school in a small community. It houses classes from kindergarten all the way through senior year in high school. This has both advantages and disadvantages. A positive is that you never had to transfer to a middle and later high school and would always be around the same people. Conversely, that also mirrored the negative aspect of being around the same people.

David sat in the far corner of the cafeteria with a few of his friends and listened to their boyish, pre-adolescent conversation with contempt. He was not into chasing girls at this point in his life. David was more concerned with how many things he could discover and was trying to figure out what he was passionate about. Just like all youth during their lives, David was trying to get an identity for himself. Each of his friends had discovered a talent that had gained them popularity and the attention of girls. Those elusive and mysterious creatures that David just could not wrap his head around the reasoning of his friends need to chase them. They made him nervous to speak to and always seemed to travel in packs, making it excruciating to approach them in any non-flirtatious conversation. David was resolute and remained aloof from most people, allowing him to enjoy private company more and people less. This resulted in him doing much of what he was doing now; listening to the nitwits he grew up with spout various obscenities and other misused nonsense that forced David to cringe often at their statements.

Because of their conversation pieces, David allowed his mind to wander and surveyed the room to seek better company. Rows of long tables adorned the wide and concrete structure. They equipped the tables with blue circular seats that were attached with metal fittings. A blue, white, and gray tiled floor supported the tables, but food stains and other unidentifiable marks marred it. They painted the walls with a dark blue on the lower three-foot of the wall and a dark gray from the three-foot mark to the ceiling. The easternmost walls, unlike the others, had a large painted picture of an eagle's head, which is the school's mascot. The doors on the eastern and western walls led outside toward the back parking lot for the seniors. David's stepsister would be in the gym, and he would have to wait for her before they both could leave for home. He glanced outside when one door opened to get an idea of what the outside looked like. He was not disappointed. From David's vantage point, he thought he could see almost two feet of snow. He hoped his stepsister's little car could make it in the rising snow.

Multiple conversations rose in buzzing waves that eventually forced the teachers to calm everyone in the cafeteria down. After waiting for what seemed like hours, the announcement of dismissal finally came, and the children and young adults began filing out. David met his stepsister at her car after bidding fairwell to his friends. They entered the car and waited for it to warm up while she talked with her classmates and some guys that flirted with her. David rolled his eyes and wondered if everything in the world revolved around base and primal instinct wrapped in a veil of education that bespoke of failed enlightenment. Still, he could say little to her of these things, for he was privy to those same base urges. Snow continued to fall in its expeditious and large flaked manner. David got uneasy with his sister's continued conversations and, knowing her driving prowess, urged her to begin the trip home. She turned and gave David a nod and bid goodbye to her classmates, then made the trip home with caution.

"I'm going to check on Uncle Homer," said David as the late eighties model Nissan Pulsar gently slid to a stop. "Would you mind letting them know where I am if I'm late?"

She stated she wouldn't mind, but reminded David not to return after dark as David ran up the road to visit his uncle. The pair would sit and talk by the fireplace for hours in the small one bedroom house. If David stayed overnight, Uncle Homer would have steaming biscuits and gravy awaiting his arrival at the breakfast table. The smell of thick-cut, smoked, maple-flavored bacon would fill the house with its sizzling aroma. Its waves of smell would permeate the small house and entice the nose to follow its tantalizing fragrance. The enticing scent of baked buttermilk biscuits wafted through the room, intertwining with the tantalizing aroma of sizzling bacon. You would flutter awake at the smell, but your eyes would glisten at the sight of the loving white biscuit blanket that wrapped the sausage like a loving partner. You would sit and wonder where to dig your fork until the unintentional happens. A large portion finds its way into your mouth and the taste buds explode in a fury of smoked bacon and fluffy ambrosia that leaves you enraptured by its taste. David thought of those times as he made his way to his great uncle's house. It had been two years since Uncle Homer had felt like cooking. He has been catching the flu a lot these last few years. Granny hired a nurse to come stay with him, but David still visited because of his amazing stories.

Uncle Homer was ninety-eight years old and had lived through and seen many amazing things. He grew up during the Great Depression and helped manage a farm and the family lands until the Army eventually drafted him during World War Two. After returning, he handled the combat stress just like any veteran. He drank it away until the bottle stopped flowing. His alcoholism eventually drove most of his family away, but after outliving all his friends, most of his family, and even some of his children, he put the bottle down. Unfortunately, the drink took its toll on his health and mental state. David was the only family that visited him regularly and he cherished him. David was the source of Homer's happiness in recent years and they both loved their time spent together.

Finally, after many musings and pondering, David arrived at his great uncle's door. He noticed Ms. Natalie, Uncle Homer's nighttime nurse, had already assumed her duties and parked in her accustomed spot in the driveway. She was a jolly older lady, with dyed brown hair cut in a shorter style that accented her jowls, that wiggled from side to side when laughing. Her rotund form would quiver with delight when Uncle Homer was in a joking mood and began a laughing fit. Overall, David delighted in her company. David raised his hand and knocked on the door and stood by while awaiting someone to answer. An eerie silence filled the house. Normally, he could hear the two laughing and cutting up. David got concerned as he heard Ms. Natalie's heavier footsteps resound through the house.

"Who is it?" Ms. Natalie questioned as she approached the door from the living room.

David responded, and she unlocked the door to allow him entry. As David entered the kitchen and continued into the living room, Ms. Natalie tenderly grabbed his arm and brought him to a halt.

"Hiya, David. Since you are the only visiting relative, I must let you know your uncle is..." she paused and took a shuddering breath. "His time is drawing near. I do not know how much time he has left, but he does not have long now. Have a brief visit today. I am sorry. Your uncle needs his rest tonight."

David's eyes widened in response, and tears exploded from his eyes. Ms. Natalie wrapped him in a tight embrace, and they stood in the kitchen, holding one another for many moments. After sharing their emotional reprieve, they composed themselves and continued into the living room where Uncle Homer lay resting. His breath remained steady, yet an unusual pallor enveloped him. David went to his side and grabbed his uncle's hand and held it. It had an odd cool feeling to it that made David want to recoil from it, but he held on. At least the VA gave him a hospital bed to aid in his comfort. The adjustable device simplified his uncle's day-to-day activities. They positioned a green couch behind the hospital bed, next to the wall and overlooking the road through a large window. To the left of the couch, a green love seat sat against the wall, with a singular end table and a table lamp separating them. A small coffee table sat between to the two seats and had a bible spread open in the middle. A thirty-two-inch screen television sat opposite the couch and played game shows. Natalie guaranteed David that he would sleep for a few more hours and would prepare him some lunch. David accepted, and the two sat and talked about some of his great uncle's stories and tales. Some of them had to do with his adventures overseas. He never spoke about what he did in the military, but he talked about the countries he had visited and some people he met. Sometimes, he would tell stories of his childhood and some things he experienced during the Great Depression. Some of his stories depicted hardship and poverty, yet a resilient community uplifted each other. The man spoke of barn dances and hayrides that would bring the people together for simple fun and fellowship. Church functions added to the excitement with Sunday morning music that sometimes entertained an instrument if a traveling pastor had one. He seldom shared other stories. Some of the most terrible and frightening things that one only imagined in their deepest nightmares occurred within the deep Appalachian Woods of his youth.

"He told me the most horrifying story I've ever heard about his past," Ms. Natalie said to David as they munched their sandwiches. David looked up and stared into the nurse's eyes with surprise, his eyebrows rising toward the top of his head and his eyes widening. "Did he ever tell you the story about the Messer family?"

"No, ma'am," David answered, taking a drink from his glass of sweet tea. David knew most of the older names from this area. Many of them either hunted with his uncle or had some other connection to him. All of them seemed to respect Uncle Homer, and he respected them the same, which resulted in them visiting him occasionally.

"He said it started when he was a boy during the Great Depression. A man named John Messer moved into the area with his wife, son, and two daughters. They purchased a plot of property that no one within the small community ever wanted to build upon. Native Americans who opposed the white settlers desecrating their burial grounds believed in a local superstition that cursed the land. Of course, that was only a rumor among the locals. This story fell on deaf ears when the Messers purchased it. They were not poverty-stricken or affluent, but John made his money working the railroads and settled on a farm for his family. The family had a fair and happy life and attended all the communal activities. They dressed in finery and attended church every Sunday and Wednesday as the doors opened. Eventually, Edith, Mr. Messer's wife, became an integral part of the Sunday school and soon instructed some of the youngest in the community on how to read, write, and do arithmetic. John found work at the lumber mill for extra cash while they started turning their soil to plant their crops for the next harvest because of the time of their arrival in November. That year, the winter was mild. Work remained steady, at least as steady as it could in those times, and it looked as if the family would prosper.

"The winter passed all within the area without but a whisper, but still left its chill within the bones of those that worked outdoors. Their boy contracted Scarlet Fever during this time. John and his wife spent almost all they had to aid the boy in his recovery of the illness. Eventually, the cost of saving the boy's life drained their remaining finances that were already taxed by the lack of income while staying with their son. John ended up losing his job with the mill and stayed home and worked on the farm. They ended up finishing the planting on time to harvest the first harvest and had a decent yield. They could trade for chickens and milk with their abundance of produce, and their son, Jeremy, looked as if he would be well enough to aid in minor tasks around the farm. As sometimes happens, another travesty hit the entire community as drought. Rains had fallen less and less when the heat of the summer dried up wells and springs. Dust from the roads and house floors clogged the nose with the arid dryness of the land.

"Another trial of hardship was in the road awaiting the Messers' arrival. Unfortunately, the drought lasted the rest of the summer until the fall rains began and the temperatures plummeted. Game was becoming scarce early that year. Some believed the animals left in search of water and more abundant foliage to sustain their diets. This action or migratory pattern did not aid in keeping the family of five from being hungry, however. Still, the family kept attending events within the community and maintained friendships that had formed upon their first arrival.

"Post-Christmas and New Year, a noticeable shift occurred in John's visiting and neighborly habits. Edith, Edna, Esther, and Jeremy visited often and acted as if all was right in the world. They rumored John found one of the secret places that are hidden deep within these mountains. It lies just beyond your beloved swimming spot, "Night Hole." An area in the darkest portions of those forests that permeates cold even in the dead of the hottest summer. That place conceals secrets. They made infernal pacts in that place.

"John discovered this section of the woods on the Eastern side of the North Carolina Mountains, which mirrored the opposite side of the mountain in Tennessee, during dusk. The man he was logging for sent him this way to further his clearing progress. John began walking this day to take a break from his coworkers and to clear his tumultuous thoughts about his starving family. His crops were meager, with the current drought continuing through the following year. Today was the last day his boss would have him working. Because of the rising costs of delivery and materials, few people that had money were spending it in those days. Mr. Murphy had to cut over three quarters of his labor force just so he would break even and not impoverish himself as well.

"Eventually, being in his thoughts and not being aware of his surroundings achieved the inevitable. His thoughts consumed him, causing him to lose awareness of his surroundings. Despite his expectation to reach his intended destination while traveling east and uphill, he ended up in North Carolina instead. He made a right-hand turn down a well-traveled trail that wound its way back toward the Tennessee side of the mountain. He walked for several hours under the sweltering heat of the summer sun. Giant trees of various species lined the trail, and small animal life scurried about in the underbrush beyond. The sun was topping its zenith in the sky, and he quickened his pace. After going ten feet further down the trail, he noticed a bone chilling cold that permeated his sweat-soaked clothes slicing into his core. Still, he continued and hoped that he would make the summit of the mountain before dark. As he continued the trail, he noticed a clearing twenty yards from his position and was off to the right of the trail. John noticed a small campfire in the clearing and a figure that was staring at him with ominous intent. Observing this sight would have been more disturbing if his teeth were not chattering out of his head from the cold.

"'Beg my pardon, friend. May I share your fire for a sit for a bit? I seemed to have traveled a bit too far over the mountain and I was just wondering if I may catch my breath for a few moments before continuing on, if you wouldn't mind the intrusion,' Mr. Messer asked the heavily clothed figure which regarded him momentarily before slightly nodding and turning its hooded head back toward the campfire.

"'It has been hard finding work these days, which I am sure you know all about, huh friend?' John asked the hooded figure, trying to see his host's face.

"An uncomfortable feeling twisted itself around in John's stomach, but he overlooked it and chalked it up as hunger pains. He sent all his earnings back to his family, leaving no money for him to buy food while he was away. He resigned to trapping and scavenging his food so his family would not have to go without, but he knew today was his last day on the job and he was worried.

"'It looks like this job is over. I hope I can find more work after today. I am afraid for my family if this joblessness continues. The draught is not helping either. We're already two-thirds into our food store,' complained John to his absent companion.

"John wrung his hands together, spreading the abundant amount of sweat that was running like a river through the crevices in his skin.

"'Perhaps I may help you, John Messer,' whispered a voice from under the shadowed folds of the hooded figure that sat across from John.

"It spoke with an almost inaudible voice, which John felt instead of heard. It sent shivers down John's spine and throughout his body but snapped his focus toward the strange speaker with an unknown force. A sliver of wonder crossed John's mind as a flitting shadow. The question of, 'How did he know my name?'

"'Times are hard, ain't they, John?'

"'Yeah. I thought the farming would offset the lack of money, but then the droughts came. Folks from church have helped us out, but they are almost as bad as we are and won't be able to continue that for long. How would you be able to help?' he looked questioningly at the figure and strained to pierce the veil of shadows to discern a face but couldn't make out discernable features that would be identifiable. 'Do you have some sort of work that I may do?'

"John thought he heard a sinister sounding snicker within the shadows but discounted it because of the blowing winds. It turned to its right as if to reach for something behind it. It stayed in that position for many moments, then turned back toward John and outstretched its right-gloved hand. The figure held the position for many moments before it shook the appendage in a frustrated manner toward John. After a brief pause, John heeded the suggestions of the obscured figure and extended his hand to receive its offering. The figure opened its gloved hand and dropped three ordinary looking black seeds in the palm of John's hand.

"'Drop these in the well, and they'll bear fruit that'll keep you fed in the times to come,' whispered the raspy voice.

"John felt like the voice within the shadows sneered, but John was desperate and willing to try anything to feed his family. He sat with the figure a few moments longer until he could not stand to be in this figure's company any longer. With evening already underway, John knew that failing to reach the summit before nightfall would force him to set up camp. That thought did not ease his mind with the strange figure sitting across from him, staring into the flames. Finally, he rose and thanked the stranger before he bid farewell and began climbing the mountain once again. He traveled the mountainside for many hours before finally reaching the road on the opposite side that traveled next to the river and to his house. All the way, he pondered the seeds the stranger gave him. He thought the meeting was far from usual and could not recall the meeting when later asked. Still, he finally made his front doorstep before midnight that evening, bedraggled and worn out. Edith greeted him with worried hugs and kisses that made the man blush with the satisfaction of the knowledge they cared for him. The loving pair discussed the night's occurrences and finally made their way to bed after a brief dinner.

"The following morning found John jobless. Worried, John cashed his meager check and gave the funds to his wife to purchase food and whatever other items they needed. While Edith and his children shopped, John walked out to the well in his backyard. Standing at the well, he gazed into its dried-out depths and sighed, feeling the dark cloud of a hopeless depression seep over him. He had a slight flash of memory of a shadowy figure that rested within the outer rim of his memory, whispering, 'Throw them in the well.'

"Before realizing his actions, the three black seeds were in his hands. Suspicious of the action, he inspected the subconscious action of his arm. The next moment, the seeds were gone, leaving John with no memory of him neither throwing the seeds in the well nor even being in his possession. Winter crept by. No work had been forthcoming throughout many months and desperation was taking hold of John. He became reclusive and refused all visitors. He stopped going to all community functions and quit going to church. All he would do was stand and stare down the well. After the snow fell and melted, John returned to the well with vaunted enthusiasm and stared into its shallow depths, awaiting something. Some occurrence that was forgotten, yet he remained vigilant while he watched the forming waters to observe the potential miracle that never came. John stayed awake for days. He stood unwavering by the well and maintained his watch like a sentry. Edith was worried about her husband. She would try to tell him away from his chosen guard, but he would only snarl at her and push her back.

"After some time, the other townsfolk did not see the family at all. One townsman and the sheriff, Jay Price, went to perform a wellness check one afternoon because of the worry of the community. They found him sitting in a rocking chair by the door with an ax lying across his lap. John murdered his family with the ax and splattered their blood throughout the house. Sheriff Price tried to talk to John, which resulted in a maniacal scream and charging the sheriff and the other townsman with the upraised ax. The sheriff shot him multiple times and killed him on the spot. Your uncle says the youngest daughter, who was visiting a friend, survived and passed the property down to her family, but no one wants to live there. Homer said that the EPA went to investigate and take soil samples because of the dead foliage around the house. He says nothing will grow within a one-acre diameter around the house. It seems everyone around these parts thinks the devil got him. What do you think, David?" Ms. Natalie asked her only audience member as she concluded the story.

David and Natalie sat for a while longer and discussed their beliefs about what could have happened regarding the Messers. Ms. Natalie offered various interesting points, but the more pragmatic David had his own thoughts. He wondered where the location of the area was and began searching his memory for any recollection that would describe the area enough for him to find it. David would think about this for many years to come. He went over and said his goodbyes to his great uncle and Ms. Natalie and began his snowy trip back to the single-wide trailer he lived.

Chapter 2

YEARS raced past David when he left his uncle Homer's house for the last time. He died a few weeks after the snows finally melted the beginning of May that year in 1993. Schools reconvened for the remaining weeks left, then dismissed for summer break. The boy soon forgot about the fantastical stories he used to listen to at his uncle's. After turning thirteen, he moved in with his father. He had enough of the consistent yelling and occasional beatings his stepfather would throw at him. He befriended a wider variety of people during this time. Others that lived in the same county but attended the other high school that was on the opposite end of town. They had deep roots within the surrounding community, as well.

David enjoyed these times when he lived with his father in the forested area of Cosby that rests at the foot of the Smokey Mountain National Park. It is an extremely tranquil area that provides peace to otherwise tortured souls. David and his friends would gather at his father's to enjoy one another's company and play music. During the summer of their teenage years, the new group of friends would sit around a campfire and regale all in attendance with stories. One story, that one of David's older friends told, sent an alarm through David's soul. He had heard this tale before, but the telling seemed so distant to him now. Where had he heard this story before? David listened, focused on the tale. All the while, he wracked his brain to joggle some memory where he heard this story. Several bits fell into place and some memories of sitting in his great uncle's kitchen took shape in the mirror of his mind's eye.

"This is the story of John Messer," David's thoughts screamed.

It is possible to observe something related to this ghost story. I wonder where this place is. I hope you can get there by driving. Some of these back roads can be dangerous, and my car does not have the best steering. David listened more intently now. He made it his mission to find the location of this mystery. He forgot about it for so long that he made himself promise to see it for himself this time before he forgot to pursue it. By this time, there would be some undeniable change in the area. At least, the terrain that surrounds the area should have changed. Perhaps the area will be more populated, or the other relatives moved there and fixed the place up?

Questions continued to assault David's mind as his friend continued the story. He had heard the tale several years before, but this time he heard a road name, "Dark Hollow Road." David knew where that was. One of his other friends that was in attendance lived off that road, and David's eyes darted to where he sat. Just to the right of the storyteller sat David's classmate and friend since kindergarten. Sam was of the muted sort. The young man spoke only when essential. He was a kind and honest sort and got a rapport with all those that knew him. He frequented the deeper wooded regions of their little hometown that could contain the knowledge that David sought. Acknowledging this, David turned his attentions back to the story of John Messer. Apparently, the family-maintained possession of the ten-acre property, or at least it never sold. Everyone in the community that had knowledge of the land would have nothing to do with the supposed cursed place. Such a sinister reputation, followed by the recent visit of the Environmental Protection Agency, repelled all potential buyers. He said that the foliage remained dead after so many years and that nothing would grow within the direct vicinity of the house, or the well.

After the night wore on, the adolescent boys meandered back toward their respective houses and rested in the blissful sleep of youthful dreams. David approached his friend, Sam, as he was getting into the red early nineties model Chevrolet Silverado and asked him to show the area their friend had spoken of earlier that evening. Upon solidifying the plan for the next day, David went back inside his house to bed, and Sam drove himself home to imitate his friend's action.

David found it difficult to sleep, for the growing anticipation of witnessing the remnants of such a weird and possible infernal story. Imagine if he uncovered the answers to the questions of those who allowed superstition to dictate their lives. What if those answers correctly mirrored the assumptions of those that populated the area and experienced the story firsthand? What if such evil was real in this world? Dark thoughts and questions such as these invaded David's dream like a calamity. Nightmares invaded his dreams of serenity, tarnishing his most joyful dreamscapes. He awakened in a cold sweat that soaked his bed sheets and left him shaking with fear. Being a person of Christian faith, David believed it possible for demonic or celestial experiences here on Earth and he wondered if he would be brave enough if they encountered such an entity during their visit. Eventually, David shook the dreaded experience off and curled himself back into his bed and drifted back to sleep, untroubled.

David awoke to a determined knock on his door the following morning and noticed Sam waiting, composed on the other side. David's father had to work that morning, and the boys had the house to themselves until they left on their trip to see the old house and the surrounding woods. They rolled a joint and began to puff and sip on a Coke while they planned the day's journey. Apparently, the road to the house was overgrown, and the rains rutted out the road, making it impossible to traverse except via horseback or all-terrain vehicle. Sam decided that the best course of action was to borrow his uncle Jeff's horse and ride up the mountain in order to exercise the animals and save money on gas. After they made the plans, the two put out their half-smoked joint to save for later and left to retrieve their horses for the trip up the mountain. Conversation was light and filled with jokes and laughter while traveling to Sam's uncle Jeff's house. They talked about some girls they had a crush on and some of the newer kids that had started this school year. They talked about the story that was told to them the night before. Sam had remained muted throughout the telling, but his facial expressions gave credence to the story being told. Obvious fear and shock crossed his face in an unmistakable look that added a dose of plausibility to its telling. Curiosity eventually got the better of David and he questioned his friend further about what he had witnessed. This line of questioning drew him further into silence. This action peaked David's curiosity more than any account of bloody stains or anything of that nature. In David's mind, a person scared into silence has something real to fear. Puzzled, David remained silent, and the pair listened to music until finally arriving at Jeff's, borrowing the horses.

The grizzled older man in his late fifties or early sixties greeted the two boys. He stood a straight six-foot tall that wore a long, bristly gray beard that extended to the belt loops of his overalls. Jeff worked on his family's farm that was passed down for the last four generations. He made his living selling and farming tomatoes and tobacco for the local stores and made a respectable living for his family of four. His two boys were running around in a rambunctious fashion, chasing chickens that the pair would never catch. The older man rolled his eyes at the youngsters while he continued to approach Sam with a genuine smile on his face. Uncle and nephew exchanged pleasantries, and Sam introduced David, making a fast new friend out of the older gentleman farmer. After Uncle Jeff heard the details of their ride, concern furrowed his eyebrows. After a few moments of silence, the older man warned the pair of teenage boys to stay away from such places.

"Places like that ain't for us. Its best you boys stay away from that place," the older man said.

The two boys looked at one another and promised they would not venture too far, then shook Jeff's hand and went to saddle and bridle the horses. The two horses they chose were sturdy looking horses. Jeff broke them in, but they still had some spirit in them, making them want to run and experience freedom, a driving force of ambition in the animal's minds. Jeff warned them to control their gallops and sprints to keep the spirited animals calmer during the trip. Sam and David mounted their steeds and began the five-mile trip up the mountain toward the rumored cursed portion of the forest.

The morning ride in June and during summer breaks from school was delightful. David sat astride his dual-colored black-and-white gelding in confidence and Sam sat upon his chestnut-brown mare, enjoying the day in its entirety. They riddled the boyish friendship with inane and ridiculous jokes and comments that were humorous to their minds, and merriment ensued at their humor. The joint was lit once more, and they completed inhaling the rest as they meandered the gravel road up the mountain, both enjoying the scenery. Birds of various colors twittered and fluttered in the trees' emerald-colored canopies and the large bushes that lined the path. Squirrels and other rodent-like woodland creatures skittered among the branches and underbrush that added to the wondrous symphonic nature of sounds that surrounded them. A northern breeze cooled their skin of the early summer warmth but was not cold. The last vestiges of winter blew themselves out early this year, leaving the native flora and fauna to flourish that was spectacular to behold. Several hours passed in this manner as the two traveled. They continued to talk and enjoy the day as they winded around the country gravel road up Halls' Top Mountain. After a few moments longer into their already long trip, Sam showed the dirt road that veered downward into the ravine ancient trees hid from view of whose bottom. David suggested a small rest for the horses before continuing and the other boy agreed and drew out a lunch of sandwiches for them and carrots for the horses. As they ate, Sam warned David of the road they were about to travel. He warned of major disrepair and rain damage had made travel difficult several months prior upon his first visit. He said to remain to the left of the trail due to jutting rocks from the bank and the ruts that were formed by the streams of free-flowing rain. Worst of all, several snows and storms from bygone years knocked some large trees onto the path that forces you to go up and around the obstacles in various places. Sam reassured David that the way was safe and well within his experience to handle, knowing that David could not ride like he did and wanted to ease his friend's fears.

After a bit more reassurance, the two mounted their horses and returned to their trip toward the cursed home of John Messer. They came to the dirt road that plunged downward and to the right into the forested ravine. The narrow dirt road allowed for only one vehicle to traverse its pathway. However, the two on horseback traveled the left side of the road in a slow, meandering manner.

Sam became more silent than usual, especially on this trip. David's friend was normally the most comfortable in the woods that surrounded his home, but this place made him seem uneasy.

David made another observation as they traveled the pathway and the gravel road they entered from receding in the distance behind them. The woods that surrounded them were still. It did not resemble the silence of prey hiding from a hunter, but the silence of a tomb. No birds graced their ears with their summer songs. No animals jumped or scampered, neither in the branches above nor in the leaves below. Even the wind ceased blowing from the northern direction that they should have felt on their backs flowing from the area between the ravine's borders. These uneasy observations affected David's horse as well. His large black-and-white mount's ears twitched backward, and he shook his head in anxiety, showing he wanted to go no further. David looked ahead and noticed Sam's mare was experiencing the same discomfort as his gelding. David questioned if the stories were true involving a potential curse. He always heard that animals had a general sense of those sorts of things and thought they should leave as well. However, his curiosity only increased as the horses' nervousness proved the potential of an entity or otherwise supernatural force present.

Sam glanced back at David with a half-smile on his face. David returned his friend's smile, showing that the two should urge their mounts and continue. Sam nodded and continued along the rutted dirt road toward the Messers'. The absence of wildlife caused anxious feelings for David. His hands sweated and his heart pounded in his ears. An odd chill crept over him as they traveled closer to their destination. He wondered at this current sensation. The sun blazed, signifying the height of a summer day. The weather forecast said the high was going to be in the upper eighties. This chill that David was feeling was perplexing and more puzzling than the absence of sound that sent a slight tingle of fear throughout his body. Sam slowed the pace of his horse because of the large oak that lay across the path twenty-five yards ahead. He turned and showed David what appeared to be a deer trail winding up the hill and around the tree. This was the path he told David about before they began their descent into the ravine, but David was no less nervous when he observed the treacherous-looking path.

David brought his horse to a brief halt and watched Sam creep up the small trail and see how his mare handled the terrain. The area was more traversable than it appeared and that notion emboldened David enough to try the trail that led around the tree. The black-and-white gelding walked up the hill, and David leaned forward to ease the burden on the horse. With caution, horse and rider met Sam at the top of the small trail and followed its narrow descent to the other side of the fallen tree. When both were safe on the dirt road, they continued toward their destination that was about one mile at the end of this road. However, the chill that David felt forced the hair on his arms to stand on end, and the appearance of goosebumps made him rub his arms with his hands. Sam felt the same profound chill and, through chattering teeth, informed David of the remaining distance and turned with frozen fingers, grasping the reins and urging his horse forward. Soon enough, the couple noticed a potential clearing in the middle of the ravine, located two hundred yards down the dirt road and at its terminus. Their mounts had become exhausted from this illogical and hazardous trip.

They frolicked with anxiety as they got closer and closer to their destination. Their ears lay flat, and their lips rolled back, exposing their large teeth. Their eyes became wide with fright, as if they observed a hungry wolf about to claim them as their meal. Soon after, they began to buck and kick. They tried anything at all possible to go back the way they came and return to the comfort of their barn stalls. Sam and David looked at one another after calming the horses down. They accustomed the two to hunting and the occasional shotgun blast from their riders. Neither boy could figure out what had spooked the horses so, but David and Sam were aware of the extreme unease they felt as well. Their parents always taught both to respect the opinions of animals, for they had a better perception of a threatening situation. The boys looked at one another with shocked looks and nodded their heads to return the horses to Uncle Jeff's and return home for the day. David managed a backward glance toward the center of the ravine as he followed Sam back down the old dirt road to the gravel road that would lead them back to Uncle Jeff's house. What he saw is what both storytellers of the Messer place described. He saw a small broken-down farmhouse that was surrounded by a perfect one-acre diameter circle of dead foliage. Another chill traveled through his already shivering body and David turned his full attentions on getting back to the gravel road as quickly as possible. Both boys felt an extreme sense of urgency that was shared by their respective mounts to expedite their pace. Within a few fearful minutes that forced both Sam and David to cast fearful glances behind them and search the trail behind for any sign of pursuer, they finally reached the gravel road that would lead them back.

Basking in the sun's warmth on the gravel road, the two boys appreciated the absence of heat in the ravine. All the joy they were feeling on their trip to the site was gone in a frozen fear that remained in their stomachs and poisoned the glorious day that housed the return trip. Sam and David sped down the road at a full sprint that allowed both gelding and mare to release the anxious energy that was felt on the old dirt road. They laughed in reluctance at the entire experience among themselves. Still, the cold lingered on their fingertips, forcing the pair to rub their hands together for warmth during the cloudless summer day. After about twenty minutes more of travel and nervous banter about what they observed, David and Sam returned to Uncle Jeff's and returned the horses to their stables. After they removed the bridles and saddles, they brushed the coats of their two mounts and secured the horses in for the day. David and Sam went to the truck and waved goodbye to Uncle Jeff as they opened the doors to Sam's truck and began the trip to return David home. David and Sam spoke little of the day's events on their way back to David's house. After coming back, David showed his appreciation to Sam and bid him farewell, then joined his father on the back porch to partake in an herbal remedy that would bring him tranquility and creative inspiration for his music. While father and son passed the joint between them, David relayed the story of the trip to the Messer house. Moments after David finished his story, his father's face became stern. He demanded that David never return there again and threatened corporal punishment if David returned. David respected his father and held a healthy amount of fear for the man, as well. The entire experience of the day shook David to the point of him forgetting about the mystery of the Messer house for many years. Days would become weeks. Months would become seasons. Eventually, years would pass, and other matters of interest would take the place of searching out mysteries and the sources of stories. The friends graduated from high school and began their separate adult journeys. David joined the military like his grandfather and father before him to open opportunities for himself that his family did not otherwise have. Eventually, he left his home behind and the mysteries they held in search of fresh adventures.

Chapter 3

DAVID spent ten years away from the home of his birth and childhood. The horror he experienced on Hall's Top in that frozen half-life of a ravine remained a distant memory to him that allowed him to relay the story to others as a ghost story. He traveled to many countries during his time in the military and experienced many wondrous things. He experienced the horrors of war that shook his very being and left mental scars that would linger with him for the rest of his life. Eventually, David returned to the home of his youth and reunited with his old friends. Upon his return, most things had stayed the same. The landscape that surrounded the area was more populated. His friends showed the weight of adulthood that weighed upon their shoulders. Yet, they were still the happy and friendly group from their earlier years.

David came home from California, his last duty station, before being discharged, on an early summer night in May. David was served with honor during his eight-year stint and was prepared to enjoy his time reintegrating back into the civilian mindset from before the military. As in the past, the group of friends and David's father visited the back porch of David's father's house to partake in their ritualistic smoking of multiple joints and storytelling. During this session, David and Sam relayed the tale of the time they went to the Messers' house. They chastised the pair with good-natured ribbing and banter about their lack of courage to continue to the house. David was still in his combat mindset and took mild offense to the claim of cowardice.

"I'll go tomorrow, by God," screamed David, daring any of his friends to doubt him.

They only laughed, and David's father rolled his eyes at his son's bravado. However, the older man knew that his son would follow through with such a proclamation and did not want to encourage the course of him returning to the cursed home of John Messer by making David angry. As the clock struck midnight, David's friends started departing and heading home. David and his father sat and discussed his time in the military and several of the port visits they had. David and his father stayed awake long into the night and into the early morning, sharing adventures and stories. That chilled ravine remained at the forefront of his mind, however, and he was already making the mental plan to return to the ravine and finish what he began in his teenage years.

The next day, David woke with the rising sun. He knew he had made plans with his friend Justin to go fishing on the river below his house this morning. David gathered his fishing gear and went to meet his friend on the riverbank. The conditions were perfect for fishing by the river. The wind blew in a cooling breeze that eased the summer heat. Clouds did not invade the azure-blue sky this day, providing a glaring light that forced one to squint their eyes to better focus. The day couldn't have been more perfect. He continued to marvel at the glorious day as he finished his task of loading the trunk of his early two thousand model blue Honda Civic with his fishing gear and service dog, Shadow, an eighty-pound lab pitbull mix. He bid farewell to his father and began the ten minute drive to Justin's and the river.

Darker clouds drifted in from the west. Cooling temperatures encouraged the fish to bite, which allowed the two childhood friends to catch multiple fish in a short amount of time. Justin and David conversed and made small talk while they caught and released the many bluegills, bass, and catfish that took the young men's bait. The old Messer house resurfaced during these conversations, gleaning a new bit of information from their talks. Justin was the great grandson of Jay Price, the sheriff that had to shoot the insane John Messer.

Justin relayed insignificant details that increased David's curiosity further than even in his youngest days. It solidified to David the decision that he would visit the Messer house first thing tomorrow. A few minutes past ten, the rains from the west blew in. The high blowing winds were bending some of the smaller poplar and pine trees that lined the bank. It also made casting a line near impossible, so the two friends bid farewell and left for their respective homes. While David drove toward his house, he pondered the trip to the Messer house in the morning while absent-mindedly scratching Shadow's neck. He finally arrived home and retired inside the house and relaxed with his dog for the rest of the day.

That evening was another sleepless night for David. His scars from battle had left him with a reoccurring nightmare that was the reason for Shadow's presence. The black lab pit mix had a white goatee and a white diamond pattern of fur on his chest. Although a timid dog, he approached his job with utmost dedication and would awaken David with a slap to the face when he had a nightmare. This evening was dreadful, which affected David by causing him to scream out commands and begin thrashing around in his bed. In instances such as these, a paw in the face would not wake David. He would awaken with eighty pounds of black dog curled on his face, resulting in minor suffocation and a plethora of screaming obscenities. After calming down with Shadow across his chest, he fell back to sleep in moments. That was an act he could not do without the dog's aid.

After the routine restless night, David arose and began preparing for his trip to the Messer house. After packing food, water, and his dog, he also retrieved his rifle from his room and loaded everything into the car and began his trip. He drove to where he remembered the location of Sam's uncle Jeff lived. Apparently, the family needed to sell their family property because of the subdivision that now sat in its place. David realized how much had changed in this small community. The thought crossed his mind that something could have changed the house. As he came closer to the subdivision, David noticed that someone had paved the old gravel road that led toward the summit of the mountain, and someone had built a new gas station to the left. David drove his car and parked on the far side of the gas station, well out of the way of any traffic. He then retrieved Shadow, his provisions, and his rifle and began his trip toward where he now hoped was the dirt road.

From his current vantage point, the road toward the Messer house should be less than a quarter mile. Subconsciously, he quickened his already fast pace that forced his dog to trot. Less than five minutes later, David arrived at the area where the dirt road used to be, but the overgrowth of foliage was all he saw. He led his dog from the road and skirted the top of the bank until he spied an overgrown trail only ten feet in front of him, guardrails blocked from view. Inspired and emboldened, he picked up his pace, resulting in both human and dog to jog down the overgrown path toward the supposed cursed house.

However, even the "blooded" combat veteran felt the same fear he felt when he and Sam visited many years ago. Shadow slowed his jogging pace to a slow trot, forcing the pair to walk. David shook his own fear because of his time in several combat theaters, but he could not ignore his battle buddy's reaction. He quivered with a fear that was easy to observe through his thin black fur. His muscles shivered as the two neared their destination, oblivious to the fact that they were passing the area where the fallen tree had laid those many years before. David's combat instincts forced trained reactions within the prior soldier, which also emboldened his service dog, and they returned to jogging down the path. Because of the memory of combat, he was aware of the absence of life within the surrounding woods that invaded the border of the road toward it.

Yet, as the house and surrounding yard came into view, Shadow dug his paws into the soft ground and would not move. By no circumstance would the quivering dog move on his own, which sobered up the bravado David had. In that moment, the bone-chilling cold overwhelmed him, leaving him aware of its presence. The cold of death permeated the air, but David no longer feared death. His shaking dog presented a dilemma, making travel even more challenging. In understanding but holding on to the mindset of completing the mission, he picked up his eighty-pound dog and carried him across his shoulders for the remaining quarter mile to the yard's edge.

As David neared the border of dead foliage that still encircled the broken-down house, Shadow began to dig, squirm, and claw until David was forced to tether him to a tree ten feett from the border of death. David's flesh crawled with the intense cold of the sunlit place. The log cabin was rotted and darkened to a sickly brownish-green color with mushroom growth dotting various areas. The roof of the house and porch were sunk inward more than before, giving the house the appearance of frowning at any potential visitor, or in this case, intruder. This unassuming house had accomplished what any insurgent had ever done in his life and gave him pause.

He did not understand why it was so difficult to take the step onto the property. Was it the unnatural cold that was apparently emitted from the area? Was it the undeniable sense, or feeling, of being watched? Was it the actions, or reactions, of his gut feelings and Shadow? Subconsciously, he loaded and cocked his AR-15 and stepped into the circle of death toward the frowning house. The quiet was almost deafening as he approached. It seemed like even the birds adjusted their flight patterns to avoid the area. From what David remembered, everything was the same as the stories and what he observed earlier in life. Still, he wanted to see if the bloodstains Justin had mentioned before were possibly there.

His body began to shake, and his rifle began to make a jingly noise as David's right foot touched the porch of the old house. Such cold as he had never experienced began to chill him to his bones, causing even his teeth to chatter. From his vantage point, thankfully for his endeavor, he could peer through the windows that flanked the door two feet from either side of the frame. The eleven o'clock in the morning sun poured through the windows, providing a clear view of the inside. As David squinted and looked through the windows, his eyes suddenly widened as they viewed darkened stains of blood splattered throughout the house. Unconsciously David jumped backwards and to the right of the porch, bringing him into a clear view of the well. Crushing cold sent David to his knees and again his eyes widened at the blackened and malformed plant life and dead rodents that surrounded the well in a sharp cornered shape that David could not identify. A feeling of fear like he had never known sent him rolling backward and to his feet. He sprinted and retrieved Shadow, and the pair ran the entire two miles back to the main road and away from the accursed place.

Later, David would relay his experience to others with the intent of relaying his belief in the possibility of the supernatural. This was often met with mockery and belittlement or such profound curiosity that David was uncomfortable giving the location of the place to anyone. People often ask him why he appeared so afraid when he was willing to disclose the rest of the information. David would only reply that he did not want to be held responsible for anyone else's safety concerning the Messer house. The blackened well that provided water to a frowning house haunted David with the knowledge that true evil may very well exist in this world. What has always been a question to the community was whether the cause was infernal or infernally inspired by the poisoning of the well, but David still wonders who was watching him and if that essence of evil will ever disperse.

"Hunting Grounds"

Chapter 1

THROUGHOUT our lives, we witness things that we cannot explain. As children we observe things through a slight lens of imagination that rules our perceptions. As we age, we tend to view things in a more pragmatic or sensible manner that provides cautious actions. However, there are things that have been experienced that have no logical nor scientific explanation for these observations. There have been several rumors of supernatural and other fantastical things within these old Appalachian woods. One of these things I overheard an old man speak of while sitting in this old diner off highway three twenty-one and enjoying my cup of coffee and cigarette.

It was a glorious fall day in East Tennessee for a drive in the mountains. Bob Perzansky chose to take this rural route back to his home in Charlette, North Carolina. He worked at the city newspaper as a reporter and assistant editor, but in his free time he enjoyed investigating local rumors and folklore. He took a puff from his cigarette and gazed toward the speaker. He was a tall man with balding gray hair. He spoke with such a poise that it indicated a confidence normally found in military members. He sat at the far northeastern corner of the diner, next to a wide window that faced the highway and a field with a forested area beyond. He occasionally glanced out the window to observe the multi-colored trees, then turned his attention back toward his audience.

The small gas station diner was sparsely populated this Saturday morning. Two-square-feet tables that seated four lined the walls on three sides of the small diner. Two sides of the diner were lined with large windows that provided views of the fields and the forests beyond with the trees' multicolored spectacle. A bar style eating area with eight green topped stools bordered the western wall against the gas station on the opposite side. The eating counter had a cash register that was operated by a middle-aged dark-haired lady that was as sweet as the tea she served. A genuine smile greeted all that passed her, and her general response was almost always followed by "Sweetie," or "Sweetheart." He smiled at the southern hospitality. It was the primary reason Bob decided to make North Carolina his home. He was born and raised in Boston, Massachusetts and had fallen in love with the overall warmth he experienced from the people of the Appalachian area. In his time living among them, he was also aware that, when riled, they could show a coldness that was beyond reproach and should by no means be inspired.

Other than the cashier, the cook, a singular server, and Bob, was a middle-aged married couple and the older gentleman. He found the server slowly sweeping the floors and wiping the almost empty diner for the second time and indicated his change of seats while awaiting his order. Bob grabbed his refilled warm coffee and moved to the second of three tables along the southernmost windowed wall and claimed his chair. He picked this spot for its scenic imagery outside and a better spot to eavesdrop on the trio's conversation, or most specifically, the older gentleman's story.

"It was my neighbor that lives down the hill and across the creek from me that first told me of the place. At first, I did not believe him until I saw it for myself," he looked sternly at the pair in front of him. "I know y'all just moved here, but that whole area in and around Black's Mountain is a place to avoid during nighttime," the older gentleman stated as the pair began to leave. They smiled and told him they would see him in the morning and paid their bill before leaving the restaurant. The man watched the two leave and shook his head before turning his attention back to his newspaper and coffee.

Moments after a bell rang, signifying the exit of the married couple, a plate of biscuits and gravy was gently laid in front of him.

"Would you like me to get you something else, sweetie?" voiced the waitress while she refilled Bob's coffee.

"No, thank you, but may I ask who that gentleman over there is?" wondered Bob, indicating the older gentleman in the corner.

"That's Mr. Zimmerman. He's a friendly widower that frequents here every morning. Can I get you anything else?" the waitress asked, obviously anxious to return to her other duties.

"No, thank you," Bob replied with a smile. The waitress returned the smile and returned to the kitchen. Bob turned his own attention to the aromatic heaven that sat in front of him. The white peppered gravy smothered two halved biscuits and laden with large chunks of sausage. This was the type of food that was good for the soul but terrible for the waistline. He smiled at his own sense of humor then began to cut pieces with his fork and eat them one at a time. Instinctively, Bob turned his attention from his meal and noticed the older gentleman standing next to him and smiling.

"You from 'round here?" he asked in a welcoming manner that was both friendly and respectful.

"No, sir. I live in Charlotte, but I enjoy the drive down three twenty-one and up the mountain. Why do you ask?" Bob said questioningly.

"It's the way you eat your biscuits and gravy. You are supposed to tear up the biscuits. My name is Ted Zimmerman; welcome to the area," he said with the smile remaining and extended his hand. "You must be from up north. Did you move here or just passing through?"

"I'm from Boston. It is a pleasure to meet you, Ted. My name is Bob Perzansky. I research local folklore and paranormal type activities. I couldn't help but overhear some of your earlier conversation with the couple that was seated across from you," responded Bob, returning Ted's smile and accepting his hand in greeting.

"Ah, you're talkin' 'bout what's up on Black's Mountain," said Ted, his face getting suddenly stern. "Are you just passing through, or are you stickin' around a bit?"

"I'm just passing through," Bob said, motioning toward the seat opposite from him.

Ted hesitated a moment then walked back to his table and grabbed his coffee cup. Then he walked to the counter and refilled his coffee, then returned to the seat that Bob previously offered.

"Alright, son, just don't go there in the dark of night after I tell you what I know and what some of the old ones say," Ted looked Bob dead in the eye as he spoke. A look of seriousness that hinted on the fact of a life or death situation splayed across his face that gave Bob a slight pause before indicating his approval. Such extreme curiosity invaded his mind at that very moment he began making plans to visit as he agreed not to do just that.

"Yes, sir! Would you mind if I took notes? For personal reference," Bob asked the older Ted.

"I would prefer everyone in creation not knowing about this place, sir. It's kinda one of those places that are best left alone," Ted replied sternly.

Noting the seriousness in the man's voice, Bob put his hands back on the table and returned to his meal while politely listening to Mr. Zimmerman's tale. His story lasted well into lunch time and the diner began to fill with customers. Bob's remaining plate of half-eaten biscuits and gravy had long gone cold. He was enraptured by Ted's story and the fact that many apparent sightings occurred over the last several generations. At least, enough that the superstitious carried on the legacy of the origin of the stories. Bob was always on the lookout for a true mystery, however, and he was always disappointed at some of these small mountain communities. All the stories he came across to this point were nothing other than some obviously explainable occurrence, or otherwise action. He often wondered if half the people he spoke with thus far could read and write. Some were still of the generation that had to help their families by quitting school and starting the work force, just to eat. Still, even that personal annoyance did not alleviate the fact that the stories he had traced to their source were only an illusion in the teller's mind. However, the responses and reactions of this gentleman to his story gave Bob a quite different impression of its validity. In Bob's mind, he made it his goal to visit and investigate this place. He wanted to visit this obviously haunted mountain and confront whatever supernatural force inhabited the deeply forested and wild area.

It was almost two in the afternoon when Ted finished his story, and Bob exhausted his normal line of questioning. The pair smiled at one another and thanked the other for their company before walking to the counter to pay their bill. It was getting more and more crowded with the lunch rush and the two men were thankful to conclude their conversation and leave the premises. Ted reminded Bob to never get caught up on the mountain at night, if he ever went, and waved goodbye as they walked their separate ways to their vehicles.

Bob's mind reeled as he put his key into his beige Honda accord to unlock its door. He opened the door and fell into the driver's seat, as if exhausted by the information he gleaned from the older Mr. Zimmerman. Hurriedly, he grabbed his notebook and pen and scribed in extreme detail the story that was just told of Black's Mountain. As he was recording the conversation he had just had with the elder local, he made up his mind to rent a hotel room for the evening and investigate the site in the morning. He finished writing down every note and detail he remembered then retrieved thirty-five cents from his center console to inform his wife of his plan. Luckily, she was used to this sort of news, and even supported his pursuits. Suspiciously, he often thought his wife may be having an affair. Sometimes her responses over the phone were indicative of such a thing, but he was rarely around her due to his job. He could not really blame her if she were. Still, the fact that he cared more for the discovery of a true mystery than the love of his wife made him laugh despite himself while he dialed his house's number.

The conversation went much as expected, concise. He explained what hotel he would be residing in for the evening, then he would return to Charlotte after his investigation. She laughingly wished him luck then abruptly hung up the phone. Bob thought he heard laughter in the background that brought a quick and slight surge of jealousy, but that feeling quickly vanished and was replaced by the curiosity that rested with Black's Mountain. He hung up the pay phone and returned to his car. He pulled back onto the highway east bound with the multi-colored trees on either side and relaxed the pressure from his shoulders. He passed the school on the left then the apple orchard that is located not but a mile from it. He thought of returning at some point to purchase those lovely ruby orbs that hung enticingly from the branches of the apple trees. However, he continued his drive knowing that two or three miles past the Foothills Parkway exit lay the Black Bear Motel. He decided to rent a room there this evening, then search the mountain at first light.

Bob arrived at the hotel and rented his room for the evening. After sorting his things, he left and traveled further east and across from the Cosby Campground to another small diner that was noted for their cheeseburgers to obtain his dinner and enjoy it in the park beyond. He sat on a bench that sat atop a hill that overlooked a raging creek overflowing with rainwater. Its white rapids intoxicated Bob with its raging watery power. Its splashing sounds created over the large rocks that lay on the bed of the creek hypnotized the watcher with its sizeable splashing waves.

A cold breeze began to blow in from the north and the sun began its downward descent behind the western mountain line indicating the time for Bob to return to his room and go over his notes for the evening. He gathered his refuse and threw it in the trash receptacle on his way toward his car. His thoughts lingered on his earlier conversation with the older Mr. Ted Zimmerman. He did not perceive the man to be an untruthful sort of person, but he was aware that some of the older generations that inhabited these parts enjoyed spinning a long ball of yarn. Bob smiled to himself at the analogy. He had spent much of his time like he spent today, conversing with random individuals and listening to their stories. It was interesting how people, such as these, could spin almost anything into a fantastical story and later indoctrinate it into local authority. Apparently, most of these stories were used to keep children and young adults from destroying or otherwise vandalizing different sites throughout the Smokey Mountains. Most had the desired effect and kept everyone from the storied places, however, curiosity often won over sense and visitors would venture to those fell places in the dark woods. That would explain the sincere seriousness that was entangled within Ted's voice and posturing.

He began to wonder if Black's Mountain, like some of the other sites he investigated, was the location of any illegal type actions or dealings. Such was often the case within mountainous communities, and this area was world renowned for its moon shining. Many of the steel owners would have their distilleries deep within the mountains and near a freshwater source. Mainly due to avoid detection from police or others that may want their individual products, but also to use the fresh and clean mountain water which aids in the smoothness of the fiery liquid. Bob resigned to try and find some of the local alcohol for his return trip after his investigation.

While deep within his musings a slight shower began to fall. It was a small rain that only succeeded in removing most of the humidity from the air and dropping the temperature, bringing a slight chill to the autumn day. He got to his car and opened the door while digging in his pocket for his car keys. After producing the jangling ring of metal, his fingers found and produced the desired length of metal and inserted it into the ignition to start his car and begin the trip to his room. His car wound its way through the narrow two-lane road that cut through the park. The dampened scenery began to sag and force some of the browning leaves from the trees. In his head he heard the warnings of Mr. Zimmerman from the diner, and it seemed as if the trees were weeping for his chosen course of seeking out the area of Black's Mountain. A sliver of doubt shadowed his mind as he began to believe the trees were weeping for the potential tragedy that could occur in such a reputably sinister area. A youngster's thoughts of being shredded by some unseen horror began to slide its icy claws of fear down his spine raking any vestige of courage that lay within.

"What could there possibly be on that mountain? Most of the story points at either a wild animal or some sort of ancient tribal curse," pondered Bob as he wound his car toward the Black Bear Inn.

After a short ten-minute drive in the misting rain, he arrived at his destination and was eager to bed down early to start the journey up Black's Mountain. First, he would peruse his notes about the story from his earlier encounter and route his path and return trip home from the site. He quickly parked the car and began removing his items from the trunk to carry them into his room. His one duffle bag made the endeavor effortless, and he entered the room of the one level motel that was located directly in front of his car. He threw his bag on the floor and turned on the small black and white television that sat on a chest of drawers.

The room was a bit outdated with its late sixty's early seventies décor. A myriad of color and design danced about the room in a dizzying display of randomness that made Bob wonder how a place such as this stayed in business. The motel itself was in terrible disrepair. Several doors were hanging on their hinges, several areas of paint touch up were required, and there was so much roof repair that needed done Bob was surprised it had not fallen in yet. Still, the rooms were clean, and the manager offered a home-cooked dinner with the cost of your room. Bob was eating this dinner of roasted chicken with garden-fresh vegetables and rolls as he sat at a small desk by his hotel room window and produced the notes he had written for examination and study.

He quickly scanned through his notes as he finished his meal. Upon completing the last bite, he rubbed the temples of his eyes with his fingertips, feeling a slight headache trying to invade his concentration. He laid his notebook down and produced a bottle of Ibuprofen from his bag. He dropped four of the orange-colored pills into his mouth and washed it down with a glass of water. Knowing that further research would bring about the dreaded migraines, he collapsed onto his bed, exhausted from trying to uncover a possible true mystery. The pain in his head began to throb with the thrumming of the rain, and he closed his eyes tight to ward off the intensity of the pain he knew would eventually come. Slowly, and just before the dancing and flashing lights of a migraine began to explode in his head, he drifted off into a somewhat troubled sleep where storied dreams began to take hold.

Chapter 2

LIKE many nights, and times before while he was investigating, Bob began to dream of the story that was relayed to him during his waking hours. He said it happened twenty years ago to a man named Bill that lived across from him. Bill told him this story while he returned from the funeral of Bill's longtime friend Robert Black, or Bobby to his friends, who was killed in a car accident and was found by the old river road. His car had flipped multiple times and had apparently thrown Bobby from his car where he landed several feet from the area of the wreck. His body was mutilated. Some said that he was mauled by a wild animal that came across the already wounded man and, being an easy kill, enjoyed the remainder of Bobby. That was all wildly speculated, though. All knew that Bobby enjoyed partaking in extracurricular party favors and that was the likely cause of the accident. Yet, those same people fell quiet when the questions of his injuries came into play.

"It was probably some mountain lion or bear," most people during that time were wanting to say, but none could prove such an attack. That occurrence happened only two weeks before the time Bill told Ted what he saw. The two ran into one another while working on their respective properties and Bill relayed his story.

"I just discharged from the Army. Bobby and I planned on meeting up and enjoying the summer day with a few doobies and beer. I wanted to drive up to the parkway and look at the mountains I missed from being stationed in Germany for so many years. My ex-wife has custody of my son, which gave me an unwanted amount of free time. So, Bobby and I decided to take in the warm autumn day and go for a drive to take in the scenery. We met at my mom's house while she was at church at ten in the morning. We ate some biscuits and gravy from Hardee's, then I dressed, and we left the house. We traveled toward Cosby along the river road and watched the sunlight dance across the placid surface. The cloudless sky and seventy-degree autumn weather made it a perfect day to ride with the windows down in his gray Camero. Music blared from the radio as we passed a joint and continued our drive. We passed the I-40 truck stop and made the right onto Wilton Springs toward the three twenty-one.

"We laughed and enjoyed the oranges, yellows, and reds the fall season brings. Our conversation eventually faded once we turned left east bound. We came to the BP gas station, grabbed some drinks, snacks, cigarettes, and refilled the gas tank before continuing our trip. We continued eastbound and up the winding road that led into North Carolina and into the National Park on the opposite side. We stopped at the restaurant within the small gas station that also coupled as a general store at the crossroads at the other bottom side of the mountain. We got a couple of cheeseburgers and parked our car at the first swimming hole at Waterville, just past the power plant. We finished our lunch and left Waterville and hit the I-40 toward the Foothills Parkway. We arrived at the top lookout at the parkway and fired up our second joint.

"We passed it back and forth and talked about what we experienced in the last few years. Much had stayed the same while I was gone, apparently, as you know it does while you serve in the military. Bobby said how himself and my other friends were doing much the same as they did before I left. I marveled at how much more I had done than those I left behind and decided to keep most of what I did to myself.

"We continued to sit and chat for a bit longer and enjoyed the panoramic view of the multicolored scenery that lined the mountainous views. I cranked the car, and we left back down I-40 east and took the Hartford exit to drive the old river road back toward mom's house. It had gotten dark by this time, and I had my bright lights on to better see down the dirt gravel road. If you have ever driven that road, you would know that on one side is the river and on the opposite are large and jutting rocks that fell from the mountain. Large trees had grown around the large boulders and the smaller surrounding trees created a densely forested terrain that spread wildly toward the interstate. The Pigeon River ran swift in this area. Large rocks on the riverbed made large rapids that run westerly at a fast pace that makes for fun tubing and rafting. On the opposite side of the river lay a few houses but it was mostly densely forested and wild.

"We drove about a mile when I thought I saw something ahead, just beyond my headlights, and I slowed and squinted my eyes to try and get a better glimpse. When I realized that there was something ahead, I mashed on the accelerator and began to quickly gain speed, so much so that the rear of my car began to slightly fishtail, drawing the attention of Bobby who was busy rolling our third joint.

"'Bill. What are you doing?' asked Bobby glancing quickly behind them at his driver.

"'Look ahead, just beyond the lights, and tell me what you see,' Bill said seriously and quite soberly.

"Bobby stared out the windshield and squinted tightly. After only a couple seconds, his eyes widened and he slowly turned and looked back at me.

"'I see red eyes,' Bobby said with a slight quiver in his voice. In response I mashed on the gas even harder, trying to get a better look at what was in front of us.

"At first, I thought it may be a bat, or some type of bird due to the height of the thing. Then I thought of how an avian creature would turn its head in that manner in flight. When I discounted that notion, I could not warrant any other explanation, and I sped up even more. When I sped up, I noticed the red eye-like orbs squinted as if in anger, then they disappeared to the left toward the river.

"I quickly came to a skidding stop and turned to look at Booby, who was staring over my shoulder and behind us.

"'Whatever that was, ran off toward the river,' observed Bobby, slightly shaken. 'And it's coming back!'

"That was all it took for me. I dropped the hammer so fast I fishtailed the rest of the way down that old river road. When I confirmed with Bobby what I saw, I never could explain what could stand almost seven-foot tall and fast enough to stay ahead of my headlights. What scares me the most is that was where Bobby was found torn apart. I wonder if the thing that we saw that night began hunting us. I'll tell you what. I 'll never drive that road at night again."

Other random dreams invaded Bob's dreams that night. Some of his wife's possible infidelity seemed to always invade his thoughts. Those negative thoughts made it difficult to get a good night's sleep and often affected his perceptions. He would make it a top priority to either fix this or divorce and be done with it. He surmised it had to do with his continued absence, but he also believed in the vows they both took.

Eventually his tossing and turning over the worry of his wife's potential sexual escapades woke him enough to cause him to throw himself out his bed irritably. He stomped to the bathroom to relieve himself and started the complimentery coffee in the small coffee pot provided by the motel. As the coffee began brewing, he lit a cigarette and began looking over his notes from the previous day.

He remembered the story that was told by Ted's neighbor in vivid clarity that spurred his curiosity of the Black's Mountain area. He began to read over his notes furiously with the intent to devour any clues or similarly enticing information that would lead to solving a mystery. He began to peruse his notes which confirmed his memory and dream until he came to the notation about what lay at the summit of the mountain. It was the location of an old graveyard that was said to be haunted. Most curiously, it lay within a two-mile radius of not only the encounter but the attack as well.

The graveyard was rumored to be the site of several Native American battles that resulted in horrendous bloodshed and death. Such an area, to the superstitious, could draw the attention of negative spirits or otherwise evil entities. Bob began to get more curious of the mountain as his coffee finished its brew cycle. He lit another cigarette and sipped his coffee while walking to the singular window that faced the small creek and away from the road.

As the sun began to rise, Bob noticed it would be another rare but glorious autumn day. It would be another multicolored balmy day apparently, and perfect for an outdoor investigation. He began to believe that this would be like any other trip into the unknown he had made before, fruitless. This would likely end up being nothing more than a wonderful hike into the woods, and it would provide a few amazing shots of some old and overgrown graveyard.

Amused by his own thoughts, Bob continued to sip his coffee as he turned to retrieve his clothes from the dresser. After showering and dressing, he finished his other ablutions and left to the lobby to get his free breakfast, then check out. After this was completed, he followed the same route, eastward on three twenty-one, on the winding three twenty-one highway mountain road. The road wound and wound up the mountain which provided a dizzying fall on the left side of the narrow road. Other than the treacherous potential of falling to your doom, it was a pleasant country ride. Bob had his windows rolled down in the warming autumn sunlight and brisk mountain air that contained some of the freezing spray from the occasional waterfall he passed on the right. Small white fluffs began to traverse the azure sky beyond the multicolored canopies of the trees and enticed a smile to Bob's once irritable face.

Thoughts of his wife drifted away as the clouds passed overhead. Many trails and pull-offs dotted the road toward the summit that led into North Carolina. Most were horse or old wagon trails that led deeper into Chestnut Mountain that he never traveled before, and made a mental note to do so eventually. Today, however, he would travel to the summit of Black's Mountain to observe the old graveyard and discern if there is truly anything paranormal that lived in those woods.

His mind began to drift toward the prospect again. He knew that some of these older people and people that grew up around here liked nothing more than to scare outsiders. He began to realize, after living among them, that this was primarily done to prevent unwanted onlookers from finding their moonshine stills. He began to wonder if this story would be the same case. Luckily, he kept a revolver in the glove compartment in his car and he would be certain to lock and load it before beginning his walk up the mountain.

However, he was still hoping to find a semblance of mystery within these deep woods. He searched for so long and put a strain on his marriage to pursue the prospect of finding proof the supernatural world existed. His hope was like a flickering candle in a tunnel of wind. His more pragmatic mind began to take over and he began to talk himself into the mindset of yet another disappointing dose of reality. The depressing knowledge that he possibly threw away the best thing he ever had to chase ghosts began to overshadow his thoughts. He reached into his pocket and drew out his cigarettes. He put one in his mouth, lit it, and drew a deep relaxing breath of the poisoning exhaust of the two-inch death stick. Still, the smoke, or action of smoking, relaxed him and he refocused on the task at hand.

He would travel to the restaurant at the crossroads that sits at the beginning of the national park. He would eat his lunch then travel under the overpass and up the mountain toward Black's Mountain. He would then park his car and walk the two-mile path to the graveyard at the summit. He would take some pictures, then drive the old river road in both directions before continuing toward his home and suspected-cheating wife. Bob rolled his eyes and snickered at the thought. His own insecurities always tried to invade his mind and influence his decisions. Today he would have to keep a sharp and clear mind if he were going to spot something potentially spectacular, or something of his darkest nightmares.

After about thirty more minutes of travel, he finally came to the area that turned the road from pavement to gravel, at the top of the mountainous road that was home to the first few feet into North Carolina from Tennessee. He continued along the way until he came to a stop at a stop sign that indicated the crossroad landmark from the story. Bob gazed to the left and across the road to view the gas station general store restaurant that 'Bill,' from the story, had stopped to grab lunch with his recently deceased friend. He too went into the restaurant and ordered the daily special, which was fried chicken with mashed potatoes, gravy, green beans, and a roll. He took his meal to-go and filled his car with gas before leaving and going to the storied lunch stop. He arrived ten minutes from the general store and found a bench on which to eat and to view the spectacular mountainous terrain and the beauty of the raging river that also pooled into occasional and random swimming holes. The absolute purity and natural beauty of this area still enchanted the Boston transplant. Most of this entire area was seemingly untouched by time, and the charm of the good that remained from days gone by were refreshing.

After many more moments of enjoying the forest and river around him while finishing his chicken dinner lunch with his sweet tea, he rose to throw away his trash and got into his car to continue to Black's Mountain. The sun had reached its zenith, signifying the time had reached midday and he would need to expedite if he were to fully investigate the area before dark. Not that he was afraid of the stories and rumors, but he truly did not want to be caught by some moonshining hillbilly while being lost in the woods.

He continued the mountain road and under the overpass and up the winding mountain gravel road. The narrow road seemed to wind on for hours due to the slow speed Bob had to travel in order safely traverse the path toward his destination. He passes only one house to his right while driving, that was said to be the home of the Price family for many years. Still, the landscape provided a scenery that was enjoyable to behold on his slow drive up the mountainside. Finally, he came to the indicated turn off that led to the dirt road, and Bob parked in a safe, out-of-the-way manner, and began to review his notes. After gathering his pistol and camera, he got out of his car and locked the door. He paused a moment, looking at the road toward the graveyard at the mountain's summit and took a steadying breath. Although the pragmatism he felt during his trip to this rumored haunted place had instilled an astounding amount of cynicism within his mind, and he stood frozen at the entrance that was the haunted wood.

Chapter 3

HE had been walking for several moments up the dirt mountain road that wound through the forests of Black's Mountain. It was like any other hiking trail, to Bob's disappointment. Life skittered and flitted about within the sunlit woods. The orange, red, and yellow leaves reflected the sunlight from the morning dew that was yet to evaporate from the warming rays. He walked in a leisurely fashion and enjoyed the natural stroll with the enthusiastic enchantment of one who was raised in the city.

Up and up, he hiked. His legs began to cramp, and he began to wonder if Mr. Zimmerman may have exaggerated the length of the walk. It felt like he traveled much farther than two miles at this point. The sun had almost reached the two o' clock position and Bob knew that night would fall in a few hours, so he quickened his pace. After about thirty more minutes of an uphill jog, Bob finally reached the summit of Black's Mountain and came within the boundaries of a large old graveyard that nature was beginning to reclaim.

Vines and wildflowers began to grow around and over the headstones, yet even the foliage seemed to respect the gravesites, leaving them untouched. Birds provided a calming song around the area that relaxed the amateur investigator. Bob smiled and relished the warm sun's glow as he produced his camera. He wandered around the gravesite for hours, taking pictures and observing the landscape and terrain. He observed a few peculiar markings on a few of the other headstones. Bob took a few ancient languages classes in college. A girl that he had a crush on at the time was into that sort of thing. Something about becoming a female "Indiana Jones" or some such. She believed that this sort of investigating would bring that sort of cinematic excitement into her real life. If she were chasing the same thing as he, she would be in for disappointment of monumental nature. He began to wonder if she was walking around old and likely empty graveyards taking pictures. However, a couple of those other headstones he took pictures of had a long dead Native American tribe symbol that adorned them. He thought he had flashes of a memory of those symbols being some sort of warning, but he shrugged those notions off.

He soon lost track of time while he tried to strain at the memory of where that symbol was from and what exactly it meant. He pondered for so long that the only thing that woke him from the reverie of his ponderings was the frightened flight of a flock of crows that headed southeasterly then quickly diverted south. This intrigued Bob, being mildly acquainted with avian natural flight patterns.

As he looked to the sky looking at the strange flight pattern, Bob also became aware of how low the sun had dipped since his arrival. It would be near impossible to reach his car before dark since the sun was setting at an obvious five o' clock. He was beginning to get anxious. He could not explain his reasoning for his acute anxiety, but he began to search his surroundings in the middle of the graveyard. He noticed nothing that was not there within the last couple of hours he was there. He was aware that the forest animals had stopped their activities since the fearful escape of the crows. Bob reflexively grabbed his pistol and began purposefully walking toward the dirt trail that led toward his car.

All the forest life activity had come to a crushing end, and Bob became acutely aware of the silence that had invaded the once lively wilderness area. Being born and raised in the city, he could only relate it to the feeling of being marked and followed for a mugging. He felt as if, even though armed, he was the prey and was grossly ill-prepared for the coming conflict that was about to befall him if he did not get back to his car.

Light was becoming a precious commodity as he began to sprint down the mountain trail. The quiet woods around him echoed with a crashing snap that originated behind and to the left of Bob from the ravine below. The sudden noise spurred his feet into a faster pace that encouraged a spray of dust in Bob's fleeing wake. Reflexively, he glanced over his right shoulder and strained his eyes in the day's fading light. Fearfully, he spied, what his mind registered, a fast-moving shadow that darted between the trees on the ravine's floor. Bob stopped his flight to see if he saw something or if his eyes were playing fearful tricks on him. He began to sweat, and he gripped the handle of his gun in a shaking and fearful grip. Another twig snapped to his right and forced Bob's legs back into expedited movement back toward his car.

He was about only a few hundred yards away from his car when he stumbled and fell to the ground. The sudden fall knocked the wind from his body and the gun from his hand. Stars began to dance before his eyes due to hitting his head on a fallen branch from a large black walnut. A low, otherworldly growl brought Bob's senses screaming back into reality and forced the dancing lights to stand still. He quickly jumped to his feet and sprinted with all the adrenaline-amplified speed and strength born of fear. He knew his gun was lost and his only form of protection was gone from him against whatever it was that was hunting him.

Within a few more fearful breaths and heartbeats, his car finally came into view within the mountain area's twilight that was filtered through the trees. Long shadows cast by the fading sun brought the illusion that many dark demons crouched and waited behind the old and longstanding forest guardians. Another growl sounded from somewhere behind the fleeing man and a whimper of fear escaped his lips. He knew he was fighting a concussion because of the dizzying nausea that tried to invade his senses, but the knowledge he was about to be mauled by some unseen primal force urged him on with an unknown constitution.

Breathlessly, he reached his car as the sun finished its descent behind the western mountain line. He shakily fumbled to retrieve his keys from his right front pocket and unlocked the driver's side door. He thought he heard his unknown predator throw caution to the wind with the knowledge of the potential of losing its quarry by the crashing of large limbs or even trees back in the direction he came from.

Quickly, he jumped into his car and thrust his keys into the ignition and started his car. He knew he could not speed down this old road for fear of colliding with another car, but he did not want his predator to catch up to him either. He locked his door and slammed his car into drive and peeled back down the road he previously traveled. He could only get up to the speed of thirty miles per hour, however, and Bob felt that this was not fast enough to evade whatever hunted him.

His fear began to get the better of him, resulting in him continuously looking out at his rear windshield to potentially spot the thing that chased him. On the top of the ridgeline on his left and to his rear, Bob thought he saw a tall figure darting between the trees, just outside the light of the only other streetlight on the mountain. Bob pushed the gas pedal down further and his car lurched as it picked up speed.

Scared with the knowledge he was being hunted by something so full of primal hatred it chased him for many miles, and the obvious concussion, he missed the turn that would have taken him down the interstate and back home to Charolette. Fearfully realizing this, he took the next right, that was the old gravel river road that Mr. Zimmerman told him of yesterday. Bob looked over his right shoulder once more and thought he saw a tallish figure dart through the rightmost side of the underpass just as he was about to make his right-hand turn. He fearfully accelerated so fast he fishtailed his car an eighth of a mile down the gravel road before regaining control of his car.

Trees loomed like grasping sentinels on the right side of the gravel road, and jutting rocks provided a perilous border. Dancing moonlight from river to the right of the road tried to entice Bob's eyes like the sirens of fairy tales lure sailors to their doom. Bob turned on his bright lights as he continued to try and escape the hellish terror that followed him from the mountain. He continually glanced up the forested barrier that flanked the gravel road hoping he would not glimpse another shadowy figure. Moments passed and nothing more happened, so Bob let off the accelerator and rolled his windows down to cool the nervous sweat that had soaked his shirt.

Still dizzy from his concussion, he saw lights ahead that indicated the end of the old river road, and he slowed his car even further to the suggested speed limit of twenty-five miles per hour. A smile of relief just crossed his face when something hit his car from the side. Bob cut his wheel to the right sharply and slammed his foot on his brakes causing his car to spin. After a few dizzying moments, his car began to right itself when his car was hit again.

This time the car tipped over the ledge leading toward the river and landed on its side, knocking Bob completely unconscious.

Sheriff Hause was doing his normal night shift patrol. He loved his job and his community, although he knew some of them were into a bit of meanness, he knew they were still good folks at heart. He was just leaving from getting his dinner from the local McDonalds in Newport when dispatch came over the horn and called him toward the old river road going toward Hartford. He thought it would likely be some drunken teenaged idiot that liked to party in those hills and ran their parents' car off the road. He shook his head and turned on his siren before taking the I-40 east exit out of Newport toward the Wilton Springs exit and old river road.

The sheriff arrived at the scene within minutes of dispatch's report. He saw a couple and another man standing next to the riverbank just beyond the overpass that was the interstate. When he got closer, he saw a Honda Accord that had flipped on its side and the passenger door had been seemingly ripped away. There were blood smears throughout the vehicle and some drops around the car, but nobody was ever found. Clawed tracks were later spotted by a local tracker that assisted in the continued report with the Sheriff, but they were muddled as if brushed away.

No one ever found Bob Perzansky. A missing person was initiated by local and some joint North Carolina officers, who aided in the search, but they were all fruitless. Ted continued to narrate the story to people about the area of Black's Mountain to whoever listened. Since he knew that the curious nature was the way with people, even when it involves things best left untouched, he decided he would sit and continue to stare at the Appalachian woods. Ted decided he would enjoy his coffee while patiently awaiting his next audience that was always willing to listen, and he smiled.

"Hook"

TWISTING and turning, he roiled and wrestled with the things that seemingly bound him like a snake coiling around its prey to an earthly prison. He violently thrashed to release himself from his confinement, but he could not. No matter how hard he tried, the binding was just too great and there was no escape. Relentlessly on and on the fight with the serpentine contender raged against its victim and then squeezed. His breaths came in laborious whimpers as the striking realization hit him: He was dreaming. Quickly, his eyes shot open, and he gazed about to make further sense of his surroundings.

Sean was in his room that faced the main road and the swimming pool in a trailer park in East Tennessee. He looked around his white-walled room that was decorated with mallard curtains, bedspread, sheets, and pillowcases. Not that he really cared for mallards, but his mother thought this was something he was into and was her pick flavor of decorative prowess, or lack thereof. He had a high standing desk that covered a large portion of the white carpeted floor and bore a multitude of comic books and cards that he enjoyed reading and looking at. A few posters of Cindy Crawford in a swimsuit were displayed on opposite walls that provided Sean with a view of his pre-adolescent crush. A chest of drawers sat against the wall adjacent to his bed and next to the door which led into the living room of the single-wide tan trailer.

Nightmares, such as the one he just had, began to invade his sleeping mind ever since his stepfather threatened with more harmful punishments as he got older, and this last one was bad. The police were called this last time. Sean's mother lied to the officers and stated that he was in an earlier fight with a neighborhood kid, and he did not like his stepfather because he was not his real father. This was not the case, however. Many abusive occurrences that involved Gerard throughout Sean's

115

youth were the result of Sean's hatred of Gerard. His actions resulted in Sean having vivid dreams that came into reality a day or two later. Dreams, such as these, occurred after specific events throughout Sean's life, and he began to meditate on them to acquire calmness.

When Gerard and his mother first began dating, Sean really liked Gerard. He once caught his mother cheating on him with another man while the two were dating but never told him. He wanted to at the time, but his young mind threw the information away as refuse and was replaced with whatever cartoon or toy that caught his attention. Yet all that changed the night after his father returned home from serving overseas in the military. Gerard began getting drunk more often and his anger would rage as he fueled the fire with alcohol.

"Where are my keys?!" Gerard screamed in a drunken stupor and spittle flew from his mouth one Sunday evening when Sean was asleep in bed.

"Gerard, he's only five and sleeping. He won't know anything about your keys." his mother began to plead.

The back and forth went on for several hours until he heard his mother scream about Gerard throwing his mother to the ground and shoving her face in the mud. He remembered his grandparents, aunts, and uncle coming to their little single-wide trailer by the river. The out of the way place where he and his mother lived at the time was cheap and affordable while his mother worked and went to school. After this incident, Gerard and Sean's mother did not see one another at the trailer for some time.

After a few months went by, the pair apparently made up. He said whatever nonsense the woman wanted to hear, and she took him back. Sean began having dreams of learning to fight and performing music in front of large crowds during this time, something he brushed off as youthful fancies, and enacted them in his daily play. Sean and his mother moved to a trailer-turned-house that was brown, just off the river road that led to his grandmother's and father's house. It was peaceful there for the first two months when Gerard was not around as much, but the time was substituted by a man named Jeff that was a dentist in the county west of theirs and forty-five minutes away.

Jeff was a child in an adult body. That was about the only thing that he and Sean could relate to. Otherwise, Sean believed that Jeff was an ignorant moron and generally greeted him with rolling eyes and shrugged shoulders. Gerard, on the other hand, inspired other feelings. They were feelings that resided on the darker fringes of a personality that those with the attributes endeavor to hide or somehow veil them. This was a similar situation with Gerard and Sean's mother.

During this time, the beatings became worse for Sean when his mother broke it off with Jeff and Gerard began to frequent the house more often. He had developed the nervous tick of licking, and picking, his bottom right lip during the months Gerard stayed with them in that little brown house. Being around his mother's boyfriend sat Sean on edge, and he began to alienate himself to his room or outside and away from the older tormentor. It was during this time the dreams of martial training came more frequently and became more vivid. He began watching kung fu movies and shows eventually became almost obsessed with martial sciences. During his outdoor play, Sean began to imagine himself bludgeoning thousands of foes with his hands and feet. He would spin through the imagined attackers with effortless fury laying the invading legions low. This sort of play eventually caught the attention of Gerard, and apparently infuriated him even more.

A few days after Gerard's observation of Sean's martial play, his mother dropped him off at a sitter's house while she was working. Sean was able to play freely at this place without catching the ire of his mother's chosen partner. He would enact his imagined and dreamed rock shows and, especially, his martial play. Sticks became swords in his hands as he thwacked trees that were imaginary ninjas that were trying to steal his family's blade, or something of that nature. Eventually the time came for Sean to be picked up from his chosen sitter for the day. He waited, patiently, while watching cartoons, for his mother, but was entirely disappointed and slightly frightened to see Gerard pull into the driveway to retrieve him.

With hunched shoulders, Sean gathered his things and said goodbye while walking begrudgingly out the door and toward the car. It was a twenty-minute car ride from "Aunt Minnie's" back toward his mother's house. She was currently in school to be a registered dental assistant and Sean had to stay with Gerard until she returned. Tonight would be her late night and she would not be home until after dark. Sean began to get nervous about this fact as he opened the door to the sky-blue Monte Carlo. The unsightly rusted thing was an abomination to behold. It had holes that formed due to rust eating away at the metallic structure. The interior had a weird musky smell that was a mixture of car oil and exhaust from the smoking vehicular atrocity. It had lost its muffler ages ago and Gerard never replaced it, probably because he liked the loud rumble it produced without it.

Sean opened the door and put his bag of toys in his lap before crossing the safety belt across his lap and chest. Gerard did not even speak to him as he entered the car. He did give him a sort of sneer that bespoke what kind of day this was going to be before his mom returned. He never understood how he always seemed to draw the man's ire. Most times Sean would only be playing and would incur some sort of punishment. It had become so common place Sean began to expect it and started to become apprehensive about returning home as time around the abusive and irritable Gerard became more frequent.

Gerard had the radio turned to the classic rock station as they traversed the winding country road toward home. The windows were rolled down which allowed the warm summer air to cool the sweat-dampened skin of the boy that had run under the shining fiery orb all day. As the trip wound on and the two began closing the distance to his house, Sean began to grow anxious. As they got nearer, Sean knew the punishments would begin. He always tried to stay out of the man's way, but Sean always seemed to find himself thrown directly in his rampaging path. Sean was becoming more restless as they turned left from Wilton Springs and traveled under the I-40 overpass and passed the truck stop. Just as it always happens when Sean gets nervous, he began to pick at his lip. Only a little at first as he gazed out the car window at the grass and trees that formed a green blurring streak as they traveled.

"Stop that," Gerard yelled and slapped Sean's hand from his mouth. Anxiously, Sean dropped both his hands into his lap and clasped his fingers together tightly to try and prevent his tick from getting him into more trouble.

The anxiety mounted in Sean as he became aware of Gerard watching him and silently daring Sean to continue his comfort mechanism. Within moments, the negative emotions were too much for Sean, and he began to stretch his bottom lip with his tongue to feel the slight pain that developed and simultaneously calmed him. Just as he relaxed his tongue and was beginning to stretch his bottom lip again, pain exploded in his mouth and on his jaw. While observing Sean licking his lip nervously, the enraged man hit the bottom of Sean's mouth while his tongue was fully extended causing the boy to bite through his exposed tongue. Blood exploded from Sean's mouth as a torrent of tears began to flow unchecked down his face.

"Shut that shit up, or I'll give you something to really cry about. If you tell your mom, it will be worse," Gerard threatened, his voice edged with anger Sean couldn't understand.

Sean sobbed for the remaining five minutes to his home and held his mouth trying to stop the blood from flowing onto his shirt and other clothes.

"Get in there and go to your room. I better not see you until dinner," Gerard yelled at the distraught youth.

Sean went into his bathroom and got some washcloths and slightly dampened them before going to his room. He understood Gerard would hurt him more if he did not do what he was told so he cowered in the corner of his room. He huddled in the corner and tried to stop his mouth from bleeding with the rags before Gerard burst into his room with a crooked smile on his face.

"Get your ass up and come eat. Stop that whining bull shit! And if you tell your mom what happened it will be worse for you tonight," the man said, leaning close to Sean's ear. His putrid odorous breath gagged Sean more than his own blood and he just nodded in frightened acquiescence.

Dinner was a forced and painful experience that evening, and Gerard made sure to force the injured youth to finish it all. This dinner was particularly difficult to devour this evening due to the massive hole in Sean's tongue and the small amount of swelling it had accrued. The boy's malady gave the kielbasa sausage, rice, sautéed onions, and peppers a peculiar iron flavor caused by the bleeding from his tongue. Sean whimpered slightly as rice began to infiltrate the opening causing a searing pain in the boy's mouth.

"What's wrong with Sean," his mother asked the other adult across from her that had consumed his fifth beer in rapid succession.

"I think he may have hurt himself while playing. Other than that, I have no idea what he may have done," Gerard looked sharply at Sean as he answered his mother, daring him to comment.

Sean remained painfully silent. He understood if he said, or did anything, he would draw Gerard's wrath later that night while he slept. A few more agonizing bites later, Sean sobbingly excused himself and went to his bedroom. Frightened beyond rationality, Sean grabbed a pillow and blanket and went to sleep in his closet with both his room and closet door shut and barricaded. Sean sat shaking in his closet for many hours as he watched the sun's rays sink below the mountains and cast their darkening shadows throughout his room. He hoped that when he fell asleep, he would not be interrupted by the screaming and violent Gerard. His eyes grew heavy as the lengthening shadows deepened and he eventually passed into the realm of dreams.

A different sort of dream began to interject itself within Sean's dreamscapes that night. In this dream, he and his mother lived back in the trailer by the river. Gerard had his mother face down on the ground and was straddling her lower back while using his bodyweight to mash his mother's face in a mud puddle. Sean felt himself scream at Gerard to stop hurting his mother, which drew the malicious man's attention, and he slowly rose from his mother's fallen body. Slowly the five-foot-nine and huskily built man sauntered toward Sean's frozen-with-fear form. Sean's instincts screamed at him to act but he remained transfixed on the murderous eyes that were glossed over and covered by the yellowing lenses of his glasses. Just as Gerard was within a few feet of Sean, the boy turned and ran. Gerard reached with a grasping hand for the boy, but Sean took a bounding step and took flight. Sean soared above his attacker and up to the treetops. He was aware Gerard was chasing him, but he was too far out of his reach, and he felt safe soaring among the tree's canopies. Sean continued his flying dream until the sun's morning rays woke him up on a beautiful summer Saturday. He crept from his room and noticed Gerard's car was gone. Relieved, he went into the kitchen to make himself some cereal and positioned himself in front of the television. He turned the dial to the channel he wanted and began to consume the animated entertainment he waited for during the week.

Sean would not encounter Gerard for a few weeks after the tongue biting incident. He went to his father's for the weekend, and the following week, and thankfully missed Gerard's conjugal visits with his mother. His time away from Gerard was lengthened by a two-week hospital stay and he was constantly surrounded by his father and other extended family that included his grandfather. Sean's grandfather was not his blood grandfather, but his step grandfather on his mother's side, and the only grandfather he knew. He and Sean developed a strong bond that was unbreakable, even now. Sean's grandfather was extremely protective of him and was also aware of the bludgeoning his grandson and stepdaughter received. This was an intuitive suspicion more than anything. Sean's mother would have him lie to his grandparents after church for family brunch and tell them she fell and hit her face on whatever she thought up at a given time. Earlier events that violently occurred between his stepdaughter and her chosen suitor, coupled with the lies of her falls, generally made his grandfather fall into a silent rage.

"That is an odd, shaped countertop bruise on your face. I've never seen one with four knuckle prints in the middle," Sean remembered overhearing his grandfather telling his mother before he went outside to play.

His mother would tell him some other lie where he would always respond with an eye roll and return his attentions to his newspaper. This would repeat the event in a biweekly repetition for several months. The same lies in the same house. To the same people. To protect the same asshole that she is still allowing to beat them. Sean took another steadying breath and continued his meditation.

A month or so went by behind the shuttered windows of the little brown house. Today was like any other bright and sunny summer day for the seven-year-old Sean. He previously had another dream of martial combat and was acting it out in his play as normal. Gerard had been to a race earlier that day and arrived at his mother's house late that evening just before the streetlights came on, indicating to Sean the time to come inside. He staggered from his Monte Carlo, roaring drunk. Sean hid behind a large oak that stood to the side opposite where the man was, and observed while Gerard lumbered toward the front door in a slobbering haze. He stayed hidden until the weaving man blundered into his mother's house and waited a few moments. He heard intense voices from the other side that quickly died down and waited a few moments more before he entered as well.

Slowly, he turned the doorknob that led into his house and peered through the door. Seeing no one inside, Sean quickly slid through the slightly opened door and quietly shut it. He hurriedly took his shoes off and darted to his bedroom and shut and locked the door. After about an hour and a half, his mother called to him to take a bath and get ready for bed. Slowly, and begrudgingly, he gathered his nightclothes and left his bedroom. He peered into his mother's bedroom that led to the master bathroom that he was told to use earlier in the week due to repairs, and noticed Gerard was gone. Sighing with relief, he went into the bathroom and ran his bath. While waiting for his bathwater to fill in the off-white rectangular tub, he expelled his mother's meatloaf from the previous day and closed the lid to the commode. He dared not flush due to him being earlier advised doing so would limit your cold water use and potentially scald you. So, Sean got in the tub and began to quickly clean himself, not hearing Gerard come back into the room and collapse onto his mother's bed.

Sean finished and dried off before exiting the tub in order to prevent a mess and potential punishment. After this was complete, he quickly dressed and picked up his dirty laundry to deposit it in the laundry hamper in the other bathroom that was under repair. After completing this task, Sean began to return to the bathroom he had previously bathed in to flush the commode and complete his deposit, but it was too late.

Gerard awoke from his drunken stupor only long enough to stumble into the closest bathroom to expel the vileness that sloshed within his stomach. As he exited the bathroom, he noticed Sean standing in the bedroom doorway frozen in fear. When Sean looked in Gerard's eyes, he saw a vehemence aimed at him that made him recoil and turned to run into his room, but Gerard caught him before he could escape. He spun Sean around by the shoulders to face him then wrapped his two meaty hands around his throat, squeezed, and lifted the boy from the ground. Sean began to gasp for air as the larger man squeezed, when suddenly Sean's mother rounded the corner and observed what was happening. Sean did not recall everything that was done or said, but he remembered Gerard quickly letting him fall to the floor when his mother saw that he was strangling her son.

"What? I play with my daughter like that all the time. We were just joking around," the mildly coherent slovenly-kept man kept repeating.

"Gerard, he thought you were going to take his life away," Sean's mother replied.

During this exchange, Sean ran to his bedroom and retrieved his small wooden baseball bat from his closet and huddled in a far corner away from the bedroom door, shaking. He heard his mother and Gerard screaming at one another from beyond the closed portal, which added to his terror. Suddenly, his mother flew through the closed door and landed only a few feet from the cowering youth. Gerard, red-faced and obviously furious, stood one foot from the fallen woman muscles flexed with anger. Sean's mother began to struggle to her feet when Gerard suddenly burst into the room and quickly closed the distance between himself and the weaker woman. Gerard grabbed her by the waist and threw her on the Captain Power bedspread that covered Sean's bed. The moment she landed, she bounced and hit her head on the wall opposite the bed and to the right of the door, causing a picture frame to release from its hanging position and split the distraught woman's head open just above her eye. Gerard pounced on his victim landing on the woman in a straddling position. Then he positioned his knees on his victims' shoulders and began punching her in the face in rapid succession.

"See what you made me do!" screamed Gerard at the beleaguered and cowering boy in the corner.

Somehow, the woman slid from under her attacker and ran toward her room, leaving the frightened Sean cowering in the corner with the enraged Gerard. Fearing Sean's mother would grab his gun, Gerard chased her. After Gerard left the room, Sean ran outside through the living room door on the opposite end of the brown house and away from Gerard. Apparently, his mother had the same idea. Sean saw his mother in her car leaving the house, and about to leave him with the murderous man again. He raced to the vehicle unnoticed while his mother and Gerard were screaming at one another incoherently. He opened the back door of the car and lightly closed the door as he entered.

The sound of the car door closing scared Sean's mother into action, and she sped down the driveway while Gerard threw rocks at the rear windshield. She drove him to his grandparents' house off, what is now, three twenty-one and stayed to explain the situation for a few moments before leaving. She was gone for many days as she left Sean, once again, with his grandparents.

Eventually, he and his mother moved to a larger city and closer to his mother's work. Sean hated it there. He did not make any friends. The people there were vastly different from those of the humbler backgrounds Sean was accustomed to. The only positive thing about it was the distance from Gerard and that he never saw him. That changed, once again, as his mother fell for the fecal vocalizations that putridly flew from his odorous mouth.

He and his mother moved back to his hometown the following year, where he stayed mostly with his grandparents, once again, for two more years. It was during this time he was enrolled into *kajukenpo* martial arts, bringing his martial play into reality. This brought him into another group of people that brought him peace and he began to be more confident in himself.

He rarely saw Gerard unless his daughter was with him, until one day his mother made the decision to move in with Gerard and his mother. Gerard made sure to let him know that he would, under no circumstance, be considered his son. Sean did not really care about the statement, nor did he see this moron as a man, let alone a father. Sean already had the best father one could ask for, though his mother rarely allowed him to visit him.

Sean did not mind this time. Being around Gerard's mother kept Gerard and his drunken anger in check, which provided a relative peace in Sean's life. He attended a different school the year before junior high school began and began making new friends within the new school. He continued with his martial studies throughout this time and began to achieve higher ranks and ability rather quickly. His instructor began to teach Sean meditations to control his anger which would enable him to view the situation and calmly decide for action. Calmly but rapidly.

The next year he went back to the school of his origin. His talent of martial combat was progressing well, and he was attending tournaments where he would yield several ribbons and trophies for his performance. Sean began socializing with Gerard's daughter's boyfriends and would eventually befriend them and became part of their high school clique while in junior high school. These things began to make life more enjoyable for Sean. He had a reprieve from Gerard's wrath for about a year and a half, until Sean's eighth grade year.

His sister and he were in a terrible head-on collision that left her horribly injured and hospitalized for several weeks. Sean had a broken collar bone and was able to check on those involved to ensure their safety. He had maintained presence of mind to go to the house near the accident site and have the woman call and inform Gerard and his mother at work. After performing this task, he went to check on his stepsister who was the only one involved to be screaming. Sean observed the dash had fallen into her lap and crushed her femur that was protruding from an eight-inch jagged gash that provided a plain view of the distraught teen's marbled inner flesh. Bits of skin and meat hung from the exposed broken bones that flapped in the wind like macabre streamers. Eventually the ambulance roared onto the scene and the EMT's began assessing all those involved in the accident. Sean and the other younger passenger in the other car were transported by ambulance to the local hospital. Due to the severity of Sean's stepsister's injuries, she was flown to the nearest emergency room, and then to the operating table to apply metal applicators to her leg and arm.

Sean's father came to stay with him throughout his stay at the hospital. His mother and Gerard stayed with his stepsister until she had almost fully healed and began her physical therapy. His mother never came to check on her son until the time came for his discharge from the hospital. She fussily drove him home and tried to gather information about the accident for their lawyers. After Sean relayed the information of his stepsister leaning over to peer inside the tape deck and crossing the centerline, his mother frowned at him. With an almost accusatory tone toward Sean, she informed him to explain to the lawyers that he simply did not remember anything.

"You want me to lie," Sean asked fuzzily while the pain medication still lingered from his hospital stay.

"Sean, you will be helping this family. Just do as I say," she said while jerking his broken arm through the arm sleeve.

Sean winced in pain, but the many years of beatings from Gerard and the years of martial arts had slightly dulled his senses of pain, or simply made him more used to the experience. Sean's previous question jogged the memory of this same question several years before. His mother made him tell the same lie to his grandparents several years before. Sean knew, in that moment, she wanted him to allow these heinous and immoral acts of lying to continue. She was grooming him to, metaphorically, sweep them under the rug and act as if nothing happened. Whatever action would eventually repeat itself, and the cycle would continue and on. Sean was getting more than sick of the cycle, and he unfortunately came to the realization his mother did not care as much for him in comparison to her own image. As silently as he could muster, he would count the years down to the month he would be able to go in front of a judge and present his case to live with his father.

Eventually the pain medication finished their round and Sean's mother provided another dose. After choking down the round pill and chasing it with water, he laid himself in bed and fell into a medicated sleep. As per usual, dreams of him trying to fly away from Gerard with a hook for a hand, and martial combat made themselves a prevalent fixture in his mind. His mother's shrill nasally voice cut through his ears waking him the following morning, effectively shattering his dream.

His mother and he were going to visit and stay with Sean's stepsister at the larger hospital that was located an hour's drive west. They arrived and Sean was left to roam around the hallway, or to ride the elevator up and down. He performed these actions for about an hour before deciding to gaze from the tenth-floor window at the river beyond. They remained there until dark before Sean began to hurt too much to bear the stay and they left to return home. This continued for a week until the hospital released her, and everyone returned home. During this period Sean would trade rooms with his stepsister, and he would take hers due to the lower center of gravity of Sean's bed. This situation would continue for about three weeks longer before the step siblings were physically able to return to their prior sleeping arrangement.

After their return to school, Sean noticed an increase in popularity after the tragedy of the accident occurred within the small school. Many macabre stories and embellishments were floating around the school about injuries that were sustained. Sean did not mind this reaction in the slightest. He welcomed the many embraces from the pretty girls that roamed the halls between classes. Eventually the stardom faded, and things began to return to normal. It was nearing the end of the school year and Sean was invited to "The Battle of Atlanta," a huge martial arts tournament. Coupled with the news for the tournament was the invitation to take the college entrance exam, or ACT, with his sister due to outstanding test scores.

"Things are starting to look up! I cannot wait until this summer. I mean, it is only March so I can make it one more year. Gerard has not really done anything in a while. Maybe he will not hit us anymore," said Sean to himself as he walked from the bus stop toward the trailer where he lived.

He developed the habit of talking to himself some years ago in response to his choice to withdraw into himself instead of facing abuse. He always chose to remain outside in the woods, or in his room with the door perpetually shut. He found that the more he remained out of sight the less he was punished for whatever the two adults in the house were angry about at the time. Yet, the past several weeks had kept the two occupied and Sean was all but forgotten. Maybe his time had finally come to have peace. A smile creased his face as he approached his home, but it was one that would be short lived in the time to come.

Sean's breathing began to come in a rapid inhalation and exhalation pattern that was indicative of his anger getting the better of him. He knew that he was nearing the end of his meditation, but these last few encounters were so anger-provoking it was difficult to reach the calmness he sought. His relaxed eyes began to flutter as he felt his consciousness begin to take over his subconscious. As he rehearsed many times with his instructor, he quickly regained control of his breathing and returned his focus toward clearing his negative thoughts.

"In, two, three. Hold, two, three, four. Out, two, three, four. Hold, two, three." he repeated mentally as he slowly forced himself to regain the focus necessary to continue his meditation.

Seemingly, this practice took several minutes to regain the mental state necessary for deep meditation, but only lasted moments. Sean's chest began to expand and contract in a slow but rhythmic pattern and his mind began the process of making peace with the violence that surrounded him. His body began to relax and eventually his mind was cleared of all static. It was as if an antenna was adjusted and cleared the picture for better viewing, and the events that led to his nightmares and bed thrashing continued.

He just arrived home and made himself a snack. His stepsister was already at the kitchen table with a teacher from the school that volunteered to help in tutoring the teen. Her aid enabled the teen to finish her classes and receive the necessary credits to graduate. An hour after Sean's arrival, and while he was in his room, he heard the rumble of Gerard's car pull into the driveway. His body shuddered as he heard the car door slam shut, indicating Gerard's return home and the potential for a violent confrontation, which incited Sean's old habit of picking his lip. Luckily, the teacher was still there, limiting Gerard's aggressive reactions. An hour after Gerard's arrival, Sean heard his mother's car door open and shut, indicating her arrival. Sean became less anxious since more people were there, which usually prevented Gerard's punishments.

Sean's mother brought pizza take-out home for dinner that evening and offered the teacher a share as she was packing away her things after the lessons were over. She politely declined and said goodbye to everyone before leaving to whatever plans she had for the evening. Gerard grabbed a few of the slices while departing for his bedroom, leaving Sean, his mother, and his stepsister to eat the meal. Sean quickly devoured three pieces and guzzled his drink before returning to his room.

As the moments, and many cartoons, passed by Sean heard the rumblings of angry voices from the other side of the bedroom door.

"You will not impress your will on me! I will come and do as I please," Gerard's voice angrily reverberated throughout the trailer.

"Gerard, stop it," Sean's mother wailed in a pleading tone that drew Sean's attention and forced him to turn his television down.

There were a few more obscenities thrown between the two of them before Sean heard a loud thump that slightly shook the trailer. He jumped to his feet and saw Gerard screaming and pointing down at something on the floor. Sean walked, unnoticed, around the small island that divided the area between the kitchen and living room. Once he crossed the small ten-foot distance he saw his mother lying on the floor covering the right side of her face with her hand. Sean grew angry at the sight and began to approach the enraged man.

"Do you want some of what your mom just got, you little faggot," Gerard mocked Sean as he began to move to meet his youthful challenger.

As the two closed the distance between one another, Gerard reached out with two grasping hands toward Gerard. It was in that moment that the years of martial arts training instinctively came to bare. With subconscious movements, Sean's arms moved simultaneously in a windmill pattern that knocked Gerard's arms wide. Quickly noticing Gerard's exposed midriff and chest, Sean drove both heels of his palms into Gerard's chest, effectively halting his advance and causing him to take two steps backward to maintain balance. Immediately after striking his opponent, he reflexively dropped into a forward stance and awaited any further attack. After this was performed, Sean stared, wide-eyed, at his hands as he realized that all he had learned would protect him now. Sean looked at the surprised Gerard and smiled in such a confident manner it caused the angry adult to pause as he began to move to attack Sean again.

"Don't you use that Karate shit on me!" Gerard screamed at the obviously prepared boy.

In anger, he turned to go toward his bedroom, leaving Sean the opportunity to hurriedly exit the small trailer. Sean sprinted from his front door toward his friend's house that was located across the road and up the hill. Sean ran to his friends because he felt safe there. This was partially due to his friend Brad's stepfather Jim. Jim was a retired Army Vietnam veteran that had befriended the young Sean a few years ago. Brad told the grizzled veteran about his friend's tumultuous and abusive home life which angered him greatly. Jim had no love for Gerard and had to be calmed down by Brad's mother. In response to Sean's tale, Jim went to his weapon room. The man kept an armory locked within his house due to his preparatory nature. He quickly exited the room and carried a rifle with a long extension attached to the front of the gun. Luckily, Brad's mother calmed the prior Army sniper from blowing a hole through Gerard's already empty head.

After about an hour Sean ran back toward his house, overcome with worry for his beaten mother. The tan trailer in the center row came in view of the running boy. Gray clouds hung thick in the sky overhead, bringing the promise of rain. He noticed Gerard's car was gone as he continued his run toward the front door of his home.

"Mom, where are you going? Are you okay? Mom!" screamed Sean as his mother's car peeled out of the driveway.

Sean watched as his mother's car turned left on the main highway toward town, and probably in search of their abuser. Sean was home alone for several hours, with no word from his mother of her whereabouts or indication of her return. He turned his attentions back toward "Highlander," for the remainder of the show before worry took over his mind. He called the first person that he knew would come and help him: his father.

Within moments of ending the phone call, his father arrived. The two sat in his father's early nineties model Nissan four-by-four and awaited his mother's arrival. Sean called his father due to the fear he had for his mother and not for the hot-tempered Gerard. Hours passed and Sean's mother finally arrived, and he began to leave his father's truck to check on his mother.

"Stay here for a minute, son, I need to have a talk with your mother," commanded Sean's father.

Sean only nodded in reply and shut the door to his father's truck, remaining inside as instructed. Sean had never heard that tone of voice from his father before, and he was slightly frightened of the potential conflict that would ensue between his father and Gerard. He could not hear what his father was saying due to the sound of the rain and the car stereo, but he could see his father's finger in his mother's face and his father acted quite angry.

As Sean's father was scolding the mother of his child for neglectful behavior, Gerard's vehicle pulled into its regular parking spot. Sean watched as Gerard came around the side facing the highway, endeavoring to stay hidden, to view Sean's father give his son's mother a verbal thrashing. He continued to watch as Gerard turned and went inside his home through the back door in order to avoid the enraged man located at his front door.

After twenty more minutes passed, Sean's father made a crude gesture with his left hand and returned to his truck. He waited several more moments outside of his vehicle before climbing inside with his waiting son.

"You're coming back home with me tonight, and through this weekend. I gave your mom time to fix this issue and explained the consequences if I must remedy this. Have you eaten?" the older man asked his son.

"Yes, sir," was all the response that Sean could give his father when he had that tone of voice.

"Do you want anything to eat while we're out? You can play video games when we get back to the house. We'll figure the rest of this out later," Sean's father smiled at him in a comforting grin that made Sean relax.

"No, sir, I'm alright. Did Mom say she was going to do something this time?" Sean asked his father.

"Son, she said she was going to, but she's said that a lot of times. We can only hope, I guess," the older man shrugged his shoulders and patted his son on the back. "Everything will come out in the wash."

Sean smiled at his father as they made a right-hand turn into his grandmother's neighborhood that coupled as his father's house. His father lived with his grandmother while he cleaned off the property he recently purchased.

"Go in yonder to your room and let me talk to Luty for a minute and I'll come get you when we're done," Sean's father instructed as they exited the car and approached the house.

"Can I still play my videogames in my room?" Sean asked his father as his father opened the door.

"Why yeah! I just thought you might want to play on the big television," he said to Sean as the pair entered the house.

"No, that's alright. I can play on my little TV," Sean said to his father as he visibly relaxed.

"Hi, Granny!" Sean yelled excitedly as father and son entered the living room.

"Well, hello, pumpkin! What are you doing here so soon in the week?" his grandmother looked at his father in askance.

"Alright, son. Go get you a drink and play your game. Luty and I have some stuff to discuss then I'll come get you after," his father said to him, smiling.

Sean gave his grandmother another loving hug then hugged his dad while virtually skipping toward his designated bedroom. He felt extremely at ease within the small community. His grandmother's little three bed-room, red-brick home, stood on a two-acre plot. All within the area had about the same cookie cutter look as the next. Each was a red brick structure that had black shingle roofing and a car port. What stood them apart was their varying sizes and the way everyone did their landscaping. It was also conveniently located directly behind the church that they attended during the weeks he was with his father. He enjoyed playing basketball with the neighborhood boys on the back side of the church and playing on the large wooden fort-like playground equipment. However, he did as he was told and went to his bedroom and played his game for a few moments before his father came inside to talk with him.

"You are going to stay with me and your granny for the remainder of this week. Are you okay with that?" Sean's father asked him as he sat on the bed next to him.

"Why yeah! Is Mom okay with that?" Sean questioned his father fearfully.

"That doesn't matter. I gave her some time to fix this. The ball's in her court," his father replied, smiling.

After the brief exchange, the two hugged and his father left for the living room and Sean stayed where he was, playing his game. The difference between being with his father and grandmother and his mother was he felt more at peace here. Sean did not keep his room door closed at this house. He did not have the fear of someone attacking him in his sleep while being in his father's care.

The night continued until Sean eventually became too exhausted from the day's events and he passed out from the mental and emotional strain. That evening, he had another of his flying nightmares, but this one had a cinematic influence from the movie trailer from "Hook." In Sean's nightmare, an enraged Gerard scraped his left hand across the wall of his room while approaching him in his bed. Frighteningly, he had a hook in the place of the appendage and was ripping the dry wall from the structure with a smile on his face that promised pain. Sean rolled from his bed and burst from the closed window, shattering the glass in all directions. Gerard leapt through the shattered portal and darted toward Sean that was lying face down on the ground.

Upon seeing his attacker give chase, he jumped to his feet and began to sprint in the direction of his friend Brad's house. As Sean began to take his third step, he bounded fifty yards before landing lightly on his left foot. He vaguely remembered he had the ability to fly in his earlier years and took another huge and bounding step that launched him even higher and further than the last. He smiled to himself as he repeated this action several times, knowing he would elude his attacker. Sean looked over his right shoulder to find Gerard's hook-wielding form quickly gaining on him. Try as Sean might, he could not gain the flight he had in his younger days, and the many years of martial combat training had become a lost and distant memory within the dreamscape reality.

Oddly enough, his pursuer disappeared, and his last bounding step landed him in a white chicken coup that had only Sean as its tenet. Gerard was forgotten in this part of Sean's dream and his only concern became escaping the overly large chicken coup that contained him. Eventually this would cause him to thrash himself awake and he would gaze around in befuddlement until he understood he was with his father and safe. He stayed with his father for the remainder of the week before returning to his mother's. Gerard was nowhere to be seen, but his daughter was there and off from her job at KFC that evening. As his father's Nissan came to a stop, he turned and looked at Sean.

"Son, if you need me, all you have to do is call and I'll be here. If he hits you again, you let me know and I will handle it, okay," his father's voice slightly quivered with concern.

"I will, Dad. But I should be okay. I was more worried for Mom," Sean replied.

Father and son embraced one final time before Sean left the small truck and went inside with his mother. She glanced at Sean with a sidelong glance that bespoke disapproval as he entered. She did not say hello nor offer any indication of her wellbeing, she only scolded Sean for involving his father. Sean's mother's actions also told him that nothing was done about the events that happened a week before. There was no retaliatory response toward his violent actions to Sean and his mother from Gerard. There was only a foolhardy acceptance of some dumbass excuse from that overgrown coward. Sean rolled his eyes and walked to his room, closing the door behind him and accepting the vigilance he would have to enact again until he returned to his father's.

He had already fallen asleep before the drunken Gerard came home from the races this night. Sean was sleeping so hard he did not hear until Gerard crashed through his bedroom door with such violent rage Sean instantly was awaken. He quickly rolled out of bed and faced his attacker, but brought up his defense too late. Upon hearing the commotion, Sean's stepsister raced the short distance to Sean's room to prevent her father from hurting him. At that same moment Gerard threw a hard right hook at the unaware youth that hit the boy square in the right jaw. Sean's head snapped to the left then everything seemed to slow down as Sean slowly turned his head to its normal position and faced Gerard. A vicious smile spread across Sean's face that forced a look of surprised fear in Gerard. Gerard turned and raced past his daughter to grab a broom and return to face the boy who was slowly stalking toward him. Sean's stepsister stepped in between them and the pressure of her hand on Sean's chest lifted the curtain of rage that veiled his vision, and he stopped.

"I'll come back and finish this when you least expect it," Gerard mockingly laughed as he walked to his bedroom.

Sean turned away from his sister and watched the cops' blue lights retreat from their residence due to the neighbors reporting a disturbance. An hour or two passed from that time and Sean went to his bathroom to wash his hands. He began to realize the water from the tap was getting warmer and warmer. He also became aware that he was feeling the warmth splatter in random spots all over his body and seemingly drench his arms in sticky fluid.

"Wait. Water isn't sticky," Sean's mind exploded his consciousness back into reality from his meditative trance.

Sean looked in absolute shock at the scene before him. His mother and stepsister coward before him with blanched white faces of terror. He looked down and saw himself covered in warm fresh blood. In his right hand was one of the hook swords he was learning to use in martial arts dripping with the wetness of its first and only kill. Gerard lay eviscerated on the bedroom floor and his body began to oddly twitch in a way that made Sean begin to laugh. Sean's laughter began to reach higher decibels and pitch when he saw the white van with the padded interior approach.

Shadows in the Dark

IT is often you hear the phrase, "Back in my day" from older generations to compare the obstacles and freedoms they were forced to endure. During the end of the 20th century, children often played within the realms of dreams and imaginations until the sky blackened into night. Our parents often warned against the lingering shadows that lay beyond the illumination of the streetlamps and porch lights. We were often told to end our play and return inside before the dark hours. I always wondered why our parents, in those days, needed television commercials to ensure they were aware of our whereabouts but always ascertained shelter during the night. Parents would warn us to never look at the forest line during the time the sun fell behind the mountains to slumber and allow its luminous sister to reign in its absence and darken the world below with the coolness of night.

"Isn't mom a little dumb for telling me that now that I am older?" I asked.

Pop lit a cigarette and looked over the rims of his glasses at me, his brows raised in speculation of disrespect. He observed my boyish curiosity, then smiled, and nodded toward Dad that reclined in his chair and sipped his sweet tea. The summer rains calmed to a gentle misting that maintained a comfortable temperature. The small country home attached provided us with a peaceful environment to continue their tradition of summertime storytelling. I was nervous my earlier question would land me in trouble, neither Pop nor Dad was lenient when it came to disrespect. Pop's smile eased my fears, and I settled back on my elbows on the porches floor. I remember the story, or history, of this warning and why it was the adult's responsibility to ensure their children's safety after dark. Even after so many years have slipped away, I warn my children into the safety of our home after the sun's rays rescind behind the mountains. The story that Pop shared dated to our hometown's earliest beginning in 1807, more than 200 years ago, and the tragedy that befell the unlucky paranormal investigator that found what he was looking for.

*****

I drove the large sky-blue car down the interstate and clicked my handheld voice recorder to document the investigation. I've heard a lot of stories in my time. Everything from ghouls and goblins to the random floating lights on Brown's Mountain beyond the densely forested peaks that provided the eastern Tennessee border. This tale was the most ridiculous, nonsensical, and boorish story I had the pleasure of investigating for my tabloid employer. The premise was infuriating and childish. "Come in before dark." "Don't stare at the tree line when the sun goes down." What prattle it is. To my estimation, this will be another ridiculous notion of weird noises that people in the area are either too ignorant, or most likely stupid, to recognize. These backwater hillbillies would believe anything they were told or written in their enlarged form of propaganda that lay on every living room corner table in this region. Of course, driving this rented Monte Carlo from the McGhee Tyson airport is no picnic, and the salesman obviously conned me out of an extra couple hundred dollars for a car without power steering and no muffler.

I drove the busy Alcoa highway and turned right onto John Sevier Highway. Judging from the shaky handwritten directions from my editor, I was to continue toward Strawberry Plains and follow the I-40 to Cosby, Tennessee located in Cocke County. I am to meet an individual by the last name of Zimmerman at a diner called "Mama's Kitchen" just off highway 32. Before leaving New York, I was informed to be wary of the area. I shrugged the warning notion off and sent it to the furthest recesses of my conscious thoughts. I have survived the inner city and grew up in Queens. What would I have to worry about around these country bumkins, other than a few toothless grins and simple-minded conversation? This will be another waste of my time, but at least I am getting paid.

138

I clicked the stop button to the recorder and laid the device in the seat. I pulled a cigarette from the soft pack located in my shirt pocket and placed it in my mouth then pressed the car lighter and waited for it to complete its heating process. After hearing the click from the car lighter, I gripped the black plastic handle and placed the small circular metallic end to the opposite end of the cigarette and inhaled deeply. I gazed at the windy road dazedly through the curling smoke from the cylindrically wrapped tobacco and returned the light to its place before turning on the car radio.

The typical songs of Phil Collins blared through the speakers as the radio played. It was like his entire repertoire was on a continual repeat at every radio station from coast to coast. Still, the landscape was gorgeous, and the scenery provided a tranquil ambiance while traveling. Emerald green leaves from the various genus of foliage along the road, provided shade from the glaring sun that remained suspended in a cloudless sky. The cooling breeze that tunneled through the vehicle added to the pleasantness of the trip as I turned right onto strawberry plains from John Sevier.

After dodging tractors, a few people on horseback, and many horrendously slow-moving drivers, I finally turned east on the I-40 interstate toward Cosby. Only in Tennessee would I be stuck in traffic with the cause being agricultural farm equipment. The drive remained pleasant, minus the frustration of the slower pace of life these people seemed to enjoy, and travel quickened, allowing the coverage of many miles in little time. I arrived at the I-40 truck stop exit and turned right, continuing to follow the road signs toward Gatlinburg. After turning on Wilton Springs Road, my eyes widened at the continual growing beauty of the landscape. Fields appeared as a vast sea of flowing tall grass that emptied into the cool mountain waters of the Pigeon River. So captivated I almost did not notice I was on a bridge that spanned the width of the beautiful body of water. Curiously, I noticed a large structure in the central portion of the river from my view to my left. I made a mental note to investigate the oddity later.

I drove for several more miles, passing farmland and surprisingly enjoying the serenity of this place that time forgot. It was like time paused for the people that lived in the community, and as an outsider looking in, they did not understand their blessing. Queens was overcrowded, infested with crime, and none of it compared to the open space that surrounds me. It's almost unbearable to try and fathom the absolute freedom that has been kept hidden from my observations. It is also oppressive. At least back home there were distinguishable boundaries. There are marked street signs, and almost everything is within walking distance of where I lived.

While lost in my thoughts, I came to a "T" intersection and turned left onto Highway 32. The twisting asphalt wound around the border of yet another clear river, but the trees were growing taller and the forest thicker in this area. It was becoming apparent that much of civilization had yet to extend to this part of the state, and fear began to knot in my stomach. I wondered at the notion; what do I have to be afraid of in this backwater community? Allowing the thought to linger for only a moment longer, I shook my head to clear the veil of confusion that clouded my thoughts and focused on the road before me.

I passed a clinic, several small businesses, and a gas station before seeing the sign that indicated my destination 1 mile ahead of me on the left side of the road. It was just past noon when I pulled into the parking lot. There was a sparse amount of people within the small diner, but they all seemed content and spoke amongst themselves good naturedly. While listening to their joyous conversations, the sense of dread that knotted my stomach eased at the sound of their unique accent.

"Can I help ye, sweetie?" asked a short lady with long dark hair.

"Yes, I am here to meet a man, one Zimmerman. He normally frequents this establishment, so I'm told," I said.

"Why sure, honey! He's over yonder in that booth facin' the road, at the end there. Would ye want me ya bring ya sumthin'?" asked the waitress.

"Do you have cheeseburgers?" I asked.

"Absolutely! Do you wanna drink and fries with that?" asked the waitress.

"Can I have a tea and those fries as well?" I asked.

"I'll get that right over to ya, sweetie. You jus' holler if ya need anything else," said the waitress.

I stood perplexed at the genuine servile nature and the joyous disposition of the woman while she worked. Booths lined the north, east, and south walls that rested beneath large rectangular windows which provided clear views of the forested mountains in the distance. The seats were covered in a brown faux leather material that was easy to clean and provided comfort to the patrons of the small diner beside the gas station. Square tables rested between the booth seats for the use of the customers while they visited and ate. Condiments, napkins, silverware, salt, and pepper were placed on each table for the convenience of those being served.

Other rectangular tables were placed in strategic positions in the diner to provide more seating for the many people that occupied the restaurant during the lunch rush. Chairs were placed around the tables, which were occupied by several conversating people of various ages. Most of these individuals were too engaged in their conversations to notice me, the outsider, standing dumbfounded in the middle of this small-town eatery. Still, I allowed my eyes to follow the directions of the waitress that indicated Mr. Zimmerman, and they rested on a tall man with longish white hair smoking a cigarette and staring out the window.

He appeared to be lost in his own thoughts as I approached in trepidation, the alarm of warning echoing through my head. A plate of half-eaten food sat in front of him while he gazed at the forests beyond the road. Mr. Zimmerman's skin appeared as tanned leather, rough and sun-scorched, through the many years spent in the Appalachian Mountains. He was modestly and humbly dressed in jeans and an old T-shirt. His longish hair was combed back from his face, and its strands drifted lazily across the back of his collar. The man appeared to have once been athletic in his youth, my editor said he was a military veteran. His military bearing was apparent, even after so many years of inactive service. A scarred and gnarled hand reached for his tall glass of iced tea, and he took a long gulp. I thought I noticed a slight smile cross his lips as he noticed my approach.

"Excuse me, sir. Are you Mark Zimmerman?" I asked.

"I am. You must be that reporter feller from up north. Did ye enjoy your trip?" asked the old man.

"Other than a few mishaps, it was not bad. May I sit and have lunch with you? I'm assuming my editor spoke with you about why I'm here?" I asked.

"Why sure, pull ye up a sit down. So y'all wanna know about the disappearances, do ye? Why does this small town hold any interest to tha likes o' you northern folks?" asked Mr. Zimmerman.

"It is not the disappearances of the people, per se, because that happens all over the world. It's how they happened that raises questions," I said.

"What can you tell me about it? I'm sure ye did some research before ye came here pokin' about," said Mr. Zimmerman.

"I know that people were reported missing as far back as 1923 in this manner," I said.

"What manner might that be?" the older man asked.

"It was reported on these accounts, there were mysteries that were baffling to many observers and investigators. Seasoned hunters and trackers said they would lose the trail, and hunting dogs would only retreat to where they came as they trembled in debilitating fear," I said.

Mr. Zimmerman put the remains of his cigarette into the ashtray next to the window furthest from the pair of visitors. The waitress sat my cheeseburger with fries and my drink on the table in front of me, then graced me with a warm smile. As she turned from our table to check on the other customers that were filing in, I thought I caught a fleeting glance of a fearful look on the waitress's face. I made a mental note of the woman distancing herself from the older gentleman before me, then turned my attention to the juicy quarter-pound patty of beef before me. The smell of charred and seasoned smoked beef caressed my senses inspiring my mouth to salivate. Its aroma mingled with the buttered and toasted bun that provided its structure. Atop the patty lay an explosion of crisp, colorful, and garden-fresh vegetables that caused me to linger upon the sheer beauty of the tantalizing meal. Gently lathered mustard and mayonnaise was smoothed upon the top portion of the toasted bun, and I smiled as I piled the two parts together and placed a toothpick in the center. I grasped the large morsel with both hands and bit into the ambrosia with ravenous intent. My eyes bulged at the explosion of flavor that graced my taste buds. The mingling of the perfectly cooked burgers spices, the acidity from the onion and tomato, the calming presence of the lettuce, and the mingling condiments were accented by the playfully sweet and spicy flavor of pickle that lingered on the fringes of my first bite.

My eyes rolled in the back of my head at the sheer ecstasy of the gustative experience when I felt a piercing sensation lance through the fantasy forcing me to drop the meaty blessing onto my plate. I grabbed my arm to search for a bug bite, or more to the point, a bee sting. I rubbed my arm several times to relieve the stinging sensation and winced when I touched the central portion of the back side of my forearm. I searched the area and noticed no clue as to what caused the pain, nor did I observe any sign of injury. Shrugging my shoulders, I took a huge gulp of tea that tasted more like syrup than tea and returned my attention to Mr. Zimmerman. The man did not appear to notice my flailing, as he was lighting another cigarette unperturbed.

What do you know of this area?" asked Mr. Zimmerman.

"Not much, other than what I just told you," I said.

"Cosby was founded back in 1807. Before the colonizers came, the area was inhabited by the Cherokee. I heard from Granddaddy that children would go missing at night during those days. The parents that knew these mountains as if they were family, would lose their progeny to the horrors that lay in these woods," said Mr. Zimmerman. "It was a tall thing made of shadow. The being had spikey protrusions all over its body and stood 6 feet in height. It has elongated appendages and fingers that extend to impossible lengths in reference to its size. The Indians say it devoured the souls of the children to prolong its life and would torment hunters that lingered in its woods by forcing them into heinous acts of evil."

"How would it do that?" I asked.

"No one knows for sure, but some of the tribesman spoke of blackened thorn pricks on the skin of their brothers," said Mr. Zimmerman.

I hurriedly clicked my voice recorder to start the interview and began voraciously eating the meal in front of me while simultaneously listening to the gravelly voice of Mr. Zimmerman. I glanced outside and noticed the sun was past its highest point, and the shadows began to drift in the opposite direction. If I am going to see this thing, I need to expedite this conversation. The older man kept talking, and I returned my attention to his story.

"The date ye mentioned. Back in 1923? That was the little Carver boy whose family owns an orchard toward Keener Hollar. We always tell our younguns not ta look at the forest line or play in the woods after dark, see," said Mr. Zimmerman.

"Why?" I asked.

"The Indians call it Nalusa Falaya. A type of shadow thing, I'd reckon," said Mr. Zimmerman.

"That sounds a bit superstitious, sir," I said.

The old man smiled, what appeared to be, a sinister hinting grin, then inhaled his cigarette deeply. His eyes narrowed and the sun glinted from his eyes, casting an odd yellow hue that sparkled briefly in his pupils then disappeared. I shook my head at the odd observation and finished my tea before he continued.

"The second that happened, was a li'l outta place," said Mr. Zimmerman.

"How so?" I asked.

"Well, one night atter church, preacher Bell went missin'. He was known to like ta hunt the woods behind his house, so they figured they'd start there. He was gone fer months until we found out he was tried and convicted of 1st degree manslaughter in Texas and put to death," said the old man.

"Did he disappear the same as the Carver boy? With no discernable tracks?" I asked.

"Why yes, he did," answered Mr. Zimmerman.

"Where was this church that the preacher first went missing?" I asked.

"Holder's Grove Church," said Mr. Zimmerman.

"How far is that from the orchard?" I asked.

"Maybe about 1 to 2 miles," the older gentleman said.

"Interesting. Were there any other differences between those two? Other than the preacher showing up in another state and going crazy?" I asked.

"Not that I know of," said Mr. Zimmerman.

"Please sir, proceed," I said.

"Now, again, the Carver boy was never found, and Preacher Bell went looney. Franky Allen had the most puzzling. Ole Frankie had a steel back in tha same holler at the head of tha creek. Most of the cops knew 'im, so he didn't really get in trouble much. One night, his wife saw him sprinting from the woods into their field in their backyard and screaming that some shadowy figure was chasing him. His wife, Sharon, I believe, ran toward him only to see him yanked back into the dark fringes of the shadowed forests he ran from. Terrified, she called the police, and they started a search party. The investigators observed the tracks of a man running from the woods then being dragged back, but the trail stopped at the tree line, as if he vanished from existence. 4 months later, he tried to set a church on fire in North Carolina durin' mass," said Mr. Zimmerman.

"Am I to believe that you think this, what? This, Nalusa Falaya is responsible for these disappearances?" I asked.

"Ye asked about the stories. I told them to ye," said Mr. Zimmerman.

Puzzled, I looked out the window to my right and noticed the sun was creeping ever closer to the horizon. The shadows lengthened since I last sent my gaze toward the emerald green and densely forested landscape beyond the road from the diner. Grasping the remnants of my iced tea and gulping it down, I returned my attention to the old man before and shuddered involuntarily. The fading light enhanced the crinkled crevices in his leathery skin. Its tanned folds accentuate the elderly man's facial bones, giving the ovular face a sinister appearance. He smiled at me with lips that seemed to reach to the lengths of this mask of evil, or was it his true self, to scrape the bottoms of his ears.

"Is there sumthin' tha matter with ye? Ye look a li'l peek-ed," said Mr. Zimmerman.

I gazed down at my hands, and noticed they trembled as if overcome by an unknown palsy. The color drained from the appendages as I looked upon them, unaware of the fear that was taking hold of the depths of my being. Identifying the source of my fear was unreasonable, and well beyond the reach of my perceptions. What was in this tea? Was my food poisoned? Fear gripped my mind in hold that was unbearable. I could not focus my thoughts or maintain a conscious grip on my surrounding environment.

The inhabitants of the small diner appeared more malevolent than the comforting and welcoming dispositions they exhibited before sitting with the old man across from me. They stared at me; the newcomer, the stranger, the man who did not belong, in abject disdain. All who sat in the small room squinted their eyes; alight with the fiery hatred that burned for all who disrupted their tranquil community. Chills ran down the length of my spine, and the cold of fear drained the remaining color from my face.

Mr. Zimmerman's face took on an eviler appearance, and he stared deep into my eyes with those yellow hued orbs of his. His eyes seemed to pierce my soul as his smile widened to more impossible lengths and he leaned forward to whisper to me.

"It looks like our meetin's over, don't it? Ye don't wanna be lost out here after dark, if ye ain't from around here," said Mr. Zimmerman.

I thought I heard a slight hiss in his voice, and the deep yellow shade that reflected in the man's eyes was more than unsettling. Nodding impotently, I struggled to my feet and threw my things in my carrying bag. Throwing the strap over my shoulder, I turned to give Mr. Zimmerman a good evening, but his unsettling appearance sped my way out the glass door and to my rental car. I started the vehicle and rumbled my way toward my hotel room off Alcoa Highway. I have a vague recollection of listening to the tape-recorded interview and making the interstate. Yet, staring at the floor just under the chair on which I stand should send alarms of warning to my conscious brain. The feel of the thick hemp necklace about my throat sings its encouragement to leap to the floor. I find it puzzling that the sound of the song is Mr. Zimmerman's voice, and the pain in my right forearm burns as fire. I feel my feet move to position the chair beneath me. Why is it so difficult to breathe?

About the Author

WD Phillips II is a horror and thriller author. He wrote the dark fantasy novel, *Missives of a Maddened Monk: Taste of Power*.

A retired combat veteran, Phillips is an accomplished musician, and he enjoys his free time staying in the woods with his dogs and his daughter.